MW00478209

SongC.R.A.F.T.

SongC.R.A.F.T.

Writing Songs In Your
Authentic Voice

SongC.R.A.F.T.
Writing songs in your most authentic voice.

Published by

©2018 Moonlit Pond Records
©2018 Left Foot Forward Productions

ISBN: 978-0-578-21140-4

Written by Nancy Beaudette & Laura Zucker
Cover and book design by Moonlit Pond Records

SongC.R.A.F.T.

Table of Contents

Forward

by Susan Cattaneo,

Award-winning singer/songwriter & Songwriting professor at Berklee College of Music

Creating art is usually a strange and magical combination of intuition and inspiration, confidence and fearlessness, repetition and experience. Songwriting takes craft AND courage, and it is rare when a book comes along that addresses both the inner and outer workings of the creative process. Nancy Beaudette and Laura Zucker have come up with a creative map that will guide and nurture the artist within. Their approach comes from a place of support and first-hand experience combined with practical and fun ways to explore and develop creative ideas.

You can really get to know people from their songs, not only who they are as artists, but who they are as humans. Like a poker "tell", a song can subtly and also not so subtly give the listener a window into that artist's soul and process. I first met Nancy and Laura at a music conference in Texas, but I didn't "meet" them in the way that one normally meets people. I met them through their songs. I was drawn in by their beautiful melodies, thoughtfully well-constructed lyrics all set against some wonderful chord progressions. From the moment their songs came into my ears, I knew the women behind these works were as special as their music. I've had the pleasure of co-writing and performing with Nancy, and I have had many long discussions with Laura about what makes songwriting such a powerful medium. Each of them has years of experience working in this crazy industry. Independently, they've coached and mentored countless songwriters. Together, they came up with this wonderful concept of Song C.R.A.F.T. which they teach as a clinic at music conferences and songwriting workshops.

Song C.R.A.F.T. is an organic approach to the creative process. Written from the heart, it contains personal experiences from these two great songwriters along with practical tools that will help get you on your way to writing great songs.

"There is a vitality, a life force, an energy, a quickening that is translated through you into action, and because there is only one of you in all of time, this expression is unique. And if you block it, it will never exist through any other medium and it will be lost."

Martha Graham
choreographer

First Things First

Welcome to SongCRAFT. What we offer in this book are a series of steps designed to help you practice the flow of creativity on a regular basis, and write in your most authentic voice. Before we begin, let's talk about why we write songs in the first place. Bono says he writes from a "deep desire to communicate", and Annie Lennox believes songwriting is the "expression of the heart, the intellect and the soul." Dolly Parton may speak for many of us when she says, "Songwriting is my way of channeling my feelings and my thoughts. Not just mine, but the things I see, the people I care about. My head would explode if I didn't get some of that stuff out."

Songwriters are collectors and chroniclers of the common stories of humanity. Love and loss, peace and war, scorn and hope are just some of the themes we express in our work. We believe our songwriting is more precious than gold and jewels! It is through song that we remember the milestones in our lives. They are time capsules aligned to each heartbreak and every Friday night of our youth, and they are communication buoys pinging reminders to seize the day and celebrate life! Our favorite songs attach themselves to our emotional DNA and stay with us our whole life long. So before we pick up a guitar, pen and notebook, is there something we can do to help us write songs that will connect more strongly with our audiences? Yes. Learn to get comfortable with vulnerability because this is where authentic dialogue resides.

Songs are food for the soul, drink for the parched spirit,

and rest for the weary mind. Our fondest hope is that one of our creations will be a warm ray of the sunshine or consolation for someone just at the time they need it most. Although songwriting is part of a creative process, it nevertheless requires training and routine. Fear and judgement are natural enemies of creativity. They can keep us from connecting to our truth, but a regular creative practice will help us find our way through these obstacles. This is where SongC.R.A.F.T. comes in.

Writing is pressure and privilege at the same time. It is risk and reward, spoil and triumph. In the chapters that follow, we will share our personal experiences and the challenges we face as working musicians and songwriters. This book is for both novice and experienced writers. We will guide you through a series of exercises designed to help remove barriers that keep you from creating your best work. So now, we invite you to join us on this odyssey of SongCRAFT.

At the end of each Chapter, we invite you to view additional content and share your experience with Nancy and Laura, and other readers in our 'Members Only' area.

https://mysongcraft.com/members/

#1-Introduction Video

"For most people a critic is one who expresses an unfavorable opinion of our work; someone who finds fault with it and demeans our effort. For our purposes, the critic is that harassing voice in your head telling you your song isn't good enough"

Calm The Critic

Finding a balance between uncertainty and self-confidence is essential for a songwriter. Like the petals on a sunflower, each similar but upon closer inspection completely different, no two songwriters approach the craft of writing, or even the act of writing, in exactly the same way. We each bring a unique bouquet of skills, qualities and experiences to the table. The inner critic, though, sneaks into our projects like pesky weeds amid the beautiful blooms. Its voice buzzes round our heads, attacking like killer bees, stinging and distracting us, defeating us. Self-doubt and feelings of inadequacy are enemies of the creative process, and they can be stealthy and tenacious. In this chapter, we will look at ways to take on the inner critic and quiet that voice once and for all.

Resistance

"The more important the call or action is to our soul's evolution, the more resistance we will feel toward pursuing it." - Steven Pressfield (The War of Art)

Fear is the adversary of creativity, but the angst is fueled by our own thoughts. If we conquer our thoughts, we conquer the fear. It's like there's a fence standing between us and our art; it is a metaphor for 'resistance'. It exists to slow us down or turn us around, to require us to knock, kick and climb - or worse, to give up, and collapse into the safety of going nowhere. Then, while we're feeling sorry for ourselves, bound up with guilt, sleeping in late or having a low-grade fever of self loathing, resistance is standing proud and adding another row of brick to the wall. But the truth is, the degree to which we experience resistance is a clear sign that we're about to do something amazing. In fact, seeing resistance as a gift is the way to beat it. Be proactive. Show up every day, no matter what, and write, paint, sing, dance and bust down that barricade for good.

Nasty Voices

As children, we learn rules. Do not walk in traffic. Raise your hand. Respect other people's property. Wear matching socks. These rules protect us from embarrassment and help keep us safe. We are taught to be deferential, modest and self-effacing. These rules shape and feed our inner critic, who silently criticizes the guy wearing plaid pants with a striped shirt, the loud women talking in a restaurant about menopause, the braggart, and the parent not watching the child about to fall off the jungle gym. Our judgment meter goes off the chart when we see people breaking the rules.

This same inner critic toys with our self worth. When someone says, "That was great!", we respond, "Oh, it was nothing," or "Yeah, but...." We call ourselves songwriters but feel like imposters, "pretend" writers, frauds. We believe the message of the inner critic when it tells us that no one will read or listen or care about our songs, or that our songs are not original or have been written already. These responses and feelings come from a place of insecurity. They diminish our efforts and tamper with our reasons for writing or sharing songs in the first place. They downplay the hard work put into the writing and performance of pieces we have unveiled to the world. Sometimes, amid the din of these voices, our own unique voice is drowned out. Or simply drowned.

We do not suggest avoiding these negative voices, because they are valuable at times. We do, however, advise keeping two thoughts in mind. The first is that we are not alone. Everyone faces unnerving doubt. Every single person engaged in a creative process from engineers and CEOs, to school teachers and medical scientists - anyone looking for solutions to specific issues in their fields - feels creatively bankrupt and utterly discouraged at some point. Arguing with the inner critic, however, only amplifies its voice. It validates and legitimizes the critic's opinion.

Byron Katie, founder of 'The Work', says, "All the suffering that goes on inside our minds is not reality, it's just a story we torture ourselves with." She suggests we ponder four questions when negative thoughts assail us: (1) Is that true? (2) What happens when I believe that thought? (3) What if the exact opposite were true? (4) Why shouldn't I [insert your work of choice here]? So, for example, if the voice says, "I'm not a good enough musician to be a songwriter," we ask, "Is that really true? Do we really not have passion, musical or poetic ability? Are our life experiences truly not interesting? Do we have no imagination?" If we believe the negative thoughts, then we are bound to give in to the critic and never give our compositions a chance to be born. We are defeated before we ever begin. But, if the exact opposite is true, that our ideas are not only valid, but brilliant, and our wisdom and understanding of love and loss and life are well founded, then we should write the songs and be proud to call ourselves Songwriters!

Nancy says: I've been writing songs since I was a little girl. Back then there was no inner voice telling me to keep quiet. I simply made up words to sing for sheer pleasure. I don't remember exactly when I started censoring my work, but by the time I got to high school, my confidence narrowed. Thankfully I had teachers who recognized the 'spark' I had for poetry and music. With their encouragement, and the support of my family, I continued down the songwriting path. My inner critic will always be part of my work, but somehow after all this time, it feels more like a partner than an enemy.

Sometimes others know you better than you know ourselves. Sometimes someone else will have the faith in you that you lack. Ideally, this will light the fire of your own faith in your abilities, encouraging you to fan those fledgling flames to success. Believing in our ability and our purpose is perhaps the most powerful gift we can give ourselves. Doubt isolates and saps us. Engaging in the creative process renews, restores and re-establishes relationship. Consider that maybe the constant gnawing, uncomfortable voice in our head is really thinking that we may just be spectacular at writing songs, (or painting signs) but we are so uncomfortable with the idea of exposing our giftedness that we confuse the message for catastrophe rather than victory. Our advice is to stop fighting it! If our shields are up and our armor always on for fear of failure or criticism, we are missing the opportunity to bring life and light to a world that desperately needs our creativity. As individuals, and society as a whole, we have been enriched for millennia by the creative offerings of artists of all kinds; maybe we could take to heart this quote from Marianne Williamson: "Our deepest fear is not that we are inadequate. Our deepest fear is that we are powerful beyond measure. It is our light, not our darkness that most frightens us. We ask ourselves, 'Who am I to be brilliant, gorgeous, talented, fabulous?' Actually, who are you not to be?"

That Song Has Already Been Written!

Nancy says: I once had a song idea that came to me while driving from Montreal to Ottawa. It would be a song about a road, about the dotted yellow lines and the thought that a road is an interesting metaphor for life's journey. Before I had any details ironed out, I heard the gong. "Dang, there are so many road songs already! Mary Chapin Carpenter wrote, 'Stones in the Road'. Bruce Springsteen's classic, 'Thunder Road'. And how could I possibly compete with the Beatles, 'The Long and Winding Road'?" A few years after I moved away from home, a place where I had lived most of my life, I felt the need to revisit writing a "road" song. I had a new emotional perspective that I could attach to the physical landscape where I was raised: missing family, aging, and a longing for simplicity. All of a sudden, my road song had wheels, and "South Branch Road" was born.

> *The South Branch Road winds and rolls/*
> *Like the river that flows by its side/*
> *I can trace the years from my birth to here/*
> *Right down the center line...*
>
> *(From the CD "South Branch Road")*

In an age of Facebook and Instagram, it is tempting to compare ourselves with our peers and measure our success and failure by what others are working on, where they are gigging, what contest they've won, all the while allowing feelings of inadequacy to creep in. What do I have to offer that has not already been considered, written, expressed. However, we cannot truly know the lives of others, only what they create for our consumption. To compare our inner lives with their created outer lives is a red herring, a waste of time. To compare is to despair. This is a problem as old as time, exacerbated by the prevalence of social media access to the publicly offered lives of others. Even Teddy Roosevelt said, "Comparison is the thief of joy."

Writers have been rewriting the same seven basic plots for centuries, yet hundreds of universal themes exist to make the stories unique. Subjects like love and loss, heartbreak, first dates, missing someone, pets, trips to the lumber yard, etc. are common to the multitude but singular to the individual. When the inner critic speaks, ask, "What unique experiences and personal details around a theme make my experience distinct, and therefore, interesting and worth writing?" When we write what we know with the emotional attachment to accompany the theme and story we are trying to tell, we experience what Anaïs Nin describes as "writ[ing] to taste life twice, in the moment and in retrospect."

Laura says: One night, after a show, a man came up to me and said, "I almost didn't come out tonight, but something told me I should. And now I know it's because I needed to hear your song, 'I'm Not Ready', about living without your

Dad. My Dad just passed away too, and that song really moved me and helped me get a little further through my pain." I know that thousands of songs about the loss of a parent have been written, but it was the song that I wrote that had a profound effect on someone else. Since that night, each day I wake up, and I think, "Maybe today is the day that I write the song that will make a difference in someone else's life." And so I keep writing.

Avoidance and Procrastination

How do we know when we are being held back by the critic? When we hear a voice saying, "I'm not good enough," or "When I finish this, I'll get to that," or "I don't really know what to write about." Sometimes, when we get a great idea, we convince ourselves it is dumb and never work out the details. Other times we think, "The junk drawer really needs to be cleaned," or "That bag of potato chips won't eat itself." These thoughts and actions are enemies to the creative flow, and we must recognize them as the thieves they are.

The decision to 'begin' is more than half the battle. If we wait for inspiration, for a crystal-clear message from heaven neatly adorned with angel feathers and celestial chimes to appear, our song may never be written. If you're not creating with the consistency you long for, ask "What's holding me back?" The long list of answers probably goes something like this: not enough time, not feeling inspired, too tired, too noisy, too long a 'to do' list, blah, blah, blah. We've all been there. And it feels lousy. The problem is that we're approaching our passion like it's a chore.

11

Like buying a gallon of paint and a roller to spiff up the living room, covering the furniture with plastic but never actually opening the "rainforest dew" to start the job. On the other hand, once you've taped the door jams and baseboards, and poured that silky amazonian color into the tray, excitement loads the roller and your vision of an "au naturale" vibe is realized. We have to start sometime, so let today be the day.

Finding extra time to implement a daily writing practice may seem impractical, but keeping the songwriter alive is priority one. Berklee College professor and author, Pat Pattison, says, "Two beings inhabit your body—you and your writer—and if you're like most people, your writer is 'lazy' and could remain blissfully asleep." His advice is to "wake up your writer early so you can spend the day together." We can wake up our writers by setting our alarms 10 minutes earlier and writing first thing in the morning.

What do we write in those ten minutes? Julia Cameron, author of "The Artist's Way," says that "in order to retrieve your creativity, you need to find it." She encourages us to do this by an "apparently pointless process" called "morning pages". When you write, fill three pages - long hand - of stream-of-consciousness writing. The pages are not meant to be artfully written. They are meant to get our hand moving across the page writing whatever comes to mind. What are the advantages? Cameron says that "by spilling out of bed and straight onto the page every morning you learn to evade the Critic (what she calls "The Censor"). Because there is no wrong way to write morning pages, "the Critic's opinion doesn't count." They record our thoughts, experiences and observations without rules or agenda to preserve memories, sharpen our senses, provide an emotional purge, and reveal insights.

Allotting time to practice, keeps the creativity cogs oiled and greased, and the conduit open to the fertile songwriter part of us. Then, we can capture our best work when inspiration does strike. Our creative desires require healthy, practical habits that will set us up for success. A rhythm of repetition and routine boosts our confidence, combats writer's block, allows us to experiment with different writing styles, and sweeps through the clutter in our minds to find clarity and peace among the daily to-do's and reminders.

So, your homework is to take on some form of daily writing practice for at least 30 days. Set alarms ten or twenty minutes earlier than usual and keep notebooks and pens on the nightstand. Write whatever comes to mind, noting daily how you feel about completing the task. Hopefully, by the end, you will have established the habit of so many successful writers, which is that they get their work done before the day gets away from them. Then you can appreciate, as J.R.R. Tolkien said, that "it's the job that's never started that takes longest to finish."

Writing Exercise: Your Unique Story

(allow yourself 15 - 20 minutes)

1) Write every detail you can remember about the view looking out one particular window of the home you grew up in. (feel

free to substitute for home another building that was important during your younger years, i.e. school, corner store, garage, church, neighbours house, etc.)

2) Next, write about the relationship between you and one person or pet or thing that shared that space with you.

3) Take the strongest memories of both 1 & 2 and attach emotions to them. How does the memory of that place and that person make you feel? Does it make your heart race or your muscles tighten? Are you content and feeling well protected? Dive into the emotion of the memory and write as much detail as you can.

Remember that exploration is key here. Take the time you need. Work through resistance. Hear your own voice.

https://mysongcraft.com/members/

#2-Calm The Critic

"My art is an attempt to reach

beyond the surface appearance. I

want to see growth in wood, time

in stone, nature in a city, and I do

not mean its parks but a deeper

understanding that a city is nature

too – the ground upon which it

is built, the stone with which it is

made."

Andy Goldsworthy,
*Sculptor, photographer and
Environmentalist*

Reach Down Deep

This is one of our favourite quotes, and artist Andy Goldsworthy nails what it means to pursue the essence of time, place or thing in his art. If you've ever lost someone close to you, you'll know too well the deep grief that accompanies loss. It forever stays lodged between each breath. It is that same rawness of emotion, be it sorrow, joy, fascination, wanderlust or world view opinion, that we seek to understand on a deeper level throughout the creative process, and have permeate our songs.

Nancy says: Hearing the Cheryl Wheeler song, "Quarter Moon" for the first time really put a lump in my throat. The song describes the tender intimacies of a long-time couple in their garden. Every line in the song rolled film in my mind. I could see my mother and father working in our garden when we were kids, planting, weeding, harvesting, chatting to one another all the while. I cried at the last verse which shows the couple growing old together, an opportunity stolen from my parents when my mom died at sixty-five.

There is an understanding among writers that a good song is really a three-minute novel. It's a great way to describe what we're trying to accomplish in just a couple of verses and a chorus. We're setting a scene, following a plot to the climax and gently delivering the finale, within a very short timeframe. Well-written songs pull us in, drawing tears and shivers with deceptive ease. There's a knack to writing a piece that will make an audience gasp or cry, or laugh and dance. If they can step into our songs, to a place where they can see themselves and remember their own unique experience, then we have created a conduit to their heart. How we connect with our own feelings about whatever moment or experience we are describing is critical to the connection our audience will feel.

In this chapter, we will look at how to find that authentic voice and how to become intimate with our thoughts and feelings.

Vulnerability Is Strength

Laura says: When I started writing songs, it was because I was unable to deny my own emotions. I had just moved 3000 miles away from home with my kids and partner, when my father died. Shortly after, my partner of 20 years left me. This all happened in the same 6-month period. I was in pain, my emotions were very close to the surface, and I didn't have to reach very far down to access my most intimate truths. "Objects in the Mirror" is about that moment when I knew my relationship was really over, hoping against hope that it wasn't true:

> *"The last box sealed and loaded*
> *with all those years of history*
> *my footsteps echoed as I reached the door*
> *Long ago decided*
> *the photographs are all divided*
> *and we don't live together anymore*

I saw you start to drive away
I wanted you to hear me say
the words you would have seen
if you'd looked back for me
Objects in the mirror are closer than they appear
I'm closer- I'm right here

Thousands of years of philosophical and spiritual thought and practice have been devoted to how we can access our feelings. In her book, "Daring Greatly", researcher and author, Brene Brown, revealed this insightful, yet simple truth about vulnerability: "Vulnerability is the core of all emotions and feelings...To believe vulnerability is weakness is to believe that feeling is weakness...It is the source of hope, empathy, accountability and authenticity." She admits, "To put our art, our writing, our photography, our ideas out into the world with no assurance of acceptance or appreciation—that's also vulnerability."

We take huge risks sharing our work with the world. It takes tremendous courage, but it's worth doing because that is where authentic connection resides, that which gives purpose and meaning to our lives. As Maya Angelou says, "There is no greater agony than bearing an untold story inside you." But how do we get in touch with those untold stories? Swami Satchidananda, the founder of Integral Yoga, says, "There's no value in digging shallow wells in a hundred places. Decide on one place and dig deep. Even if you encounter a rock, use dynamite and keep going down. If you leave that to dig another well, all the first effort is wasted, and there is no proof you won't hit rock again." Sometimes it takes a stick of dynamite to mine through the layers of granite sandwiched between the head and the heart. We can become quite skilled at insulating ourselves from unnecessary pain, avoiding intense memories for fear of feeling overwhelmed. The writer's job is to peel back calloused layers of time and distance to find the beating emotion at the heart of the story.

Laura says: It took me two years after my father died to write a song about him. I thought a lot about writing it, but I could never actually get myself to sit down and do it. I knew it would be difficult to face that well of pain. So I dipped my toe in, and started writing from a distance about who he was to me:

> *"He was kind, he was strong*
> *Ready with an off-key song,*
> *or a joke that always took too long*
> *I can't see him gone"*

Rather than high dive into the deep end, I took a first step and wrote about the first truth I could access:

> *"I'm not ready*
> *I'm not ready to live without him in this world*
> *I'm not ready*
> *I'm not ready*
> *I'm only still my Daddy's girl"*

I was reluctant to face my feelings of loss, but once I worked through to the first level, it became easier to access those intensely held emotions, like digging through the earth and rock to let the aquifer's water bubble up.

It's normal for us to avoid difficult emotions. But when we explore the frozen tundra in the back of our minds we carve tunnels and shovel paths that lead to the front door and the warm hearth of ideas that await on the inside. As we chip away at the ice, the chisel may slice a nerve we cannot ignore. When we expose the raw, unadulterated emotion of a situation and experience, only then can we bleed all over the page and understand, as Brene Brown shares, that "vulnerability is not about fear and grief and disappointment...it is the birthplace of love, belonging, joy, courage, and creativity."

Our Choice of Language

The challenge now is to find the right words to express emotions in a vivid yet practical way.

Writing with the method of "show me" rather than "tell me" will put us on that path. "Tell me" is when the writer simply states how he/she is feeling, like "I can't get you out of my mind". "Show me" is like Emily Saliers' line in her song 'Ghost', "You come regular like seasons, Shadowing my dreams". She invites the listener into the place and the experience by using dynamic language, creating a more visual or visceral response. Joni Mitchell could have sung, "I'd forget you if I could, but everything about you is still part of me, and I can't get enough," but instead, she wrote "You're in my blood like holy wine, you taste so bitter and so sweet, Oh I could drink a case of you, darling and still I'd be on my feet, I would still be on my feet."

Which of these following two lyrics paints a more complete picture for you?

"I'm on my way to somewhere
Not sure where that place will be
My heart is filled with longing
I wish you were here with me
I feel so alone now
Though there are people all around
No one knows the pain I feel
I'm broken and run down" - by the authors

OR

"My heart is on the baggage-rack
It's heavy as can be
I wish that I could find someone
Who would carry it for me;
Just to pay it some attention
And to handle it with care
Because it has been dropped
And is in need of some repair."

(Excerpt from "Southbound Train" © 1991 Julie Gold)

We wrote the first example to give an honest statement of loneliness and heartbreak, but it lacks the hues and texture that allow a listener to roll the film. Julie Gold, on the other hand, brilliantly invites us into her heartache by cleverly comparing her heart to a piece of luggage, heavy and scuffed up. We can all see that bag. We can all identify with the anguish she's feeling because she made it vividly tangible. How do we learn to do this? We use language that invites the reader to connect with our subject in a more tangible way. There are many literary devices that we can practice using, with volumes of writing devoted to them. Below we've included a few tools with brief explanations of their value and an example of their use:

Imagery: ways to help the reader "visualize" ("lush soft crimson petals gently unfurling against the dewy green foliage of the rose")

Simile: comparing two different objects using "like" or "as" (My love is like a red, red rose...")

Metaphor: comparing two different objects without "like" or "as"; a word or phrase for one thing that is used to refer to another thing to show or suggest that they are similar ("Love is a rose but you better not pick it...")

Personification: comparing an inanimate (non-living) object with a person; attribution of personal qualities; representation of a thing or abstraction as a person or by the human form ("In the dawn's early light a rose awakens opening its petals to receive the morning light")

Alliteration: Using several words with the same first initial, like a tongue twister ("red, red rose")

Onomatopoeia: words that sound like what they mean: ("ouch")

We need to be meticulous with the language we use to convey the song's essense in the most concise way. Brevity is not only the soul of wit, but also of effective songwriting. One's frame of reference, however, is critical to keep in mind. Remember the old optical illusion, "Is it a vase or two faces?" Positive vs. negative space reveals that people seeing the same thing may interpret it differently. Similarly, the "Which line is longer?" illusion where a line of equal size looks longer in one figure than it does in another informs us that people seeing the same thing may interpret it differently if given two different contexts.

Two writers will create different songs about the same subject matter, as Nancy said in her example of writing a 'road' song in Chapter One. Our perspectives are unique, so let's explore one way of developing our language to support those respective vantage points.

Writing Exercise: (allow yourself 5 minutes for each part)

Part One: Describe an object. Take one thing off your person, (out of your pocket, purse, wallet, etc.) and put it on a table. Describe it. For example, here is a description of a pen and a twenty dollar bill.

> *Example: A yellow pen, spring loaded. Malala quote written on the side in white letters that says, "One child, one teacher, one book, one pen can change the world". Nobel Peace Center. Brand name 'Biotic Pen'. Memoir, journal, diary. Embossed symbol of a leaf. Pocket clip. Blue ink. Light, yet has weight in my hand. Medium tip. Newspaper ink smell.*

Part Two: Find a second object and repeat.

> *Example: Twenty dollar bill, US currency. Andrew Jackson. Federal reserve. Crisp yet worn corners. Registration numbers. Legal tender. In God We Trust. Signatures. A picture of the White House. Mine to spend wherever I want. Half a gas tank. Scratch cards. Bank account. Buy new music. Sounds crumply between my fingers. Smells like perfume. Security. Real or counterfeit. Andrew has nice wavy hair:)*

Part Three: Now describe in sentence form the two objects as they relate to one another. In the case of our example, we ask, "how does the description of a pen change when it is seen from the vantage point of a twenty dollar bill, and what happens to the money when it is understood in reference to the pen?"

Example: Twenty strokes of a pen and you sign your life away / Money has changed the world and lightened my pocket / A white house doesn't guarantee purity / Be careful the money clip in your pocket doesn't spring for the next round / Stock tips are just leaves in the wind / Enough ink to write for twenty miles / I've got the counterfeit blues / You can't brand God / Scratch your eyes out of the photo - then draw pointy ears /

Get the picture? The way we see things is steeped in the narratives we hold about them. Sometimes all it takes is viewing an object in a different context to fundamentally change the way we see that object. When you see a straight pin, you might think it will be used to sew a hem on a pair of pants, but when you see the same pin in a voodoo doll, it takes on a very different meaning. Sometimes a tea kettle is just a tea kettle, but what is it when you see it with a bottle of pain medication? Perhaps it becomes the comfort you need when you're sick. Maybe it's the arthritis in your knees screaming like the kettle whistle with each step.

Object Mapping

Object mapping is a way to elaborate visually on our thoughts and feelings towards a particular subject. The approach is non-linear, one that engages our analytical and artistic brain processes at the same time. The purpose is to collect information and explore relationships between ideas, objects, subjects. The map can take many forms – a tree trunk with branches, twigs and leaves, or a spider web with a central starting point and woven strands circling the page. Resist the temptation to simply write in columns! Mapping is a tool that can help us organize and understand information better, and assist us in translating our thoughts in image form.

For instance, here is a map of the yellow pen and twenty dollar bill.

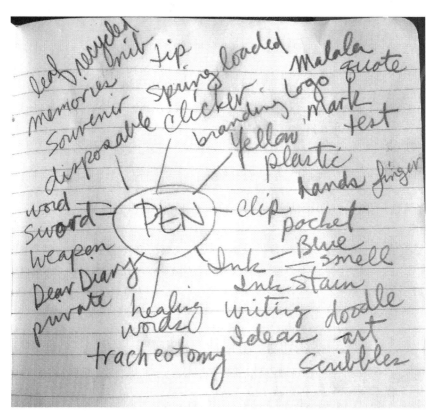

Mapping Exercise: Now it's your turn to try mapping.

Part One: This is a continuation of the exercise we did in Chapter One. Draw two circles. Write the word "home," (or the variable you used in Chapter 1) in one circle, and in the other write the name of a person, pet or thing that you associate with that place. Using either the branching or webbing style explained above, write every descriptive word that comes to mind about each subject.

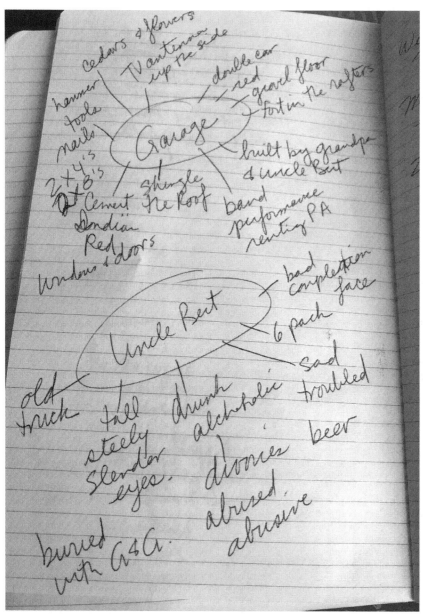

See the author's examples below:

Nancy says, The subjects I selected for this exercise were 'garage' and my 'Uncle Bert'. My Uncle was the youngest of eleven children born and raised on a farm. His was a hard luck story of wayward living and bad choices. Many tried to help him, but alcohol was his best friend. I didn't know him well, and was quite young when he and my Grandfather built our garage. I have a number of vague memories of him and interactions with the family. What I remember most is my father's kindness towards him; an

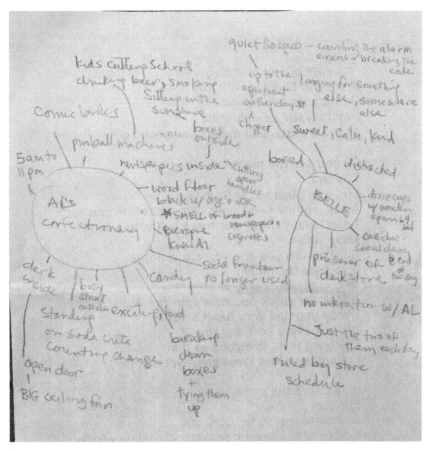

observation that has had a lasting impression.

Laura says, My grandparents owned a newsstand and candy store for many years, in Perth Amboy New Jersey. It was on the corner, with those big wooden newspaper boxes out front. Inside, there were more papers, but also a soda fountain, lots of candy, cigars and cigarettes. The back wall was covered by a huge rack holding every imaginable comic book and magazine. And to the side, in the back, three pinball machines. It was a kids' paradise. They had no employees, and were open from about 5am to 11pm. I used to visit often and stay overnight. I didn't really realize at the time that my grandparents were pretty much chained to that place. In retrospect, it was obvious that they each longed to have a different type of life, especially my Gramma Belle.

Part Two: Next, using some of the words written to describe "the place" write a line or two about the person. For example, the relationship with a brother could be that "he was my safe place, a solid wall for me to lean on," or "I trusted him as much as I trusted the loose, crooked stairs going out the back door." Then use the words written to describe the named person to write a line or two about the house. For example, "Her comforting glance was like a well-worn chesterfield, old and familiar," or "His charm dangled like a string from a bulb in a cold, moldy cellar."

Nancy's Example

"We cut down two soft maples to make room for a double car garage. We didn't know we'd be cutting into the pain of a broken man at the same time."

"Two by fours framed the wall and the rafters were hoisted on the shoulders of a weak man."

"On the outside, he was tall and slender. Inside his guts rusted like nails."

"He carried a blame that was not his to shoulder."

"The foundation was deep but the weight of his world was too much to bear"

"Shingles nailed row by row, each swing of the hammer solidified his fate"

Laura's example

"Her spirit was worn down, dimmed and dirty as the wooden floor blackened by a thousand footsteps out the door."

"Each day like the other, mind-numbing, her eyes gazing off, she's humming a tune that takes her somewhere far above those crowded counters."

"Newspapers came in in bundles, old cardboard boxes out the same way; she kept her dreams in a tiny bundle inside."

Part Three: Your Unique Story Continued

Find a quiet corner, free of distraction. Sit comfortably and be still. Take deep breaths in through the nose, and slowly exhale from the mouth. Sink into the chair, feel the body giving in to gravity, and notice the rise and fall of the lungs as the air moves through them. Slowly return to a normal breathing pattern, count to ten with each inhale and exhale, and repeat. Once totally relaxed, pick up a notebook and stream write about the following:

Think about your childhood home, (or a specific place from your past), the rooms of the house, the smell in the kitchen, the arrangement of furniture, the decor. How old are you? What are you wearing? Look for the details and write them down. How are you feeling? Who are you with? Why is this person (or thing) significant? How has the person shaped you or influenced your life? How do you feel about that person? Do you get physically stressed or emotionally capsized? Or do you feel calm and protected? What did it feel like to live in that house? If you could change something from back then, what would it be? If that person were to walk into the room right now, what would you say?

End the stream-writing by asking yourself what it would be like to walk in the front door of that home today? Then allow other questions to come forward, and keep writing until the alarm goes off. With eyes closed, take a few deep, calming breaths, and gently bring awareness back into the room.

Did any new information surface? Did anything unsettling come up? Were there tears or a grin? Was there shivering or goosebumps? Perhaps a gentle nudge, an invitation to probe deeper into a memory bubbled up. Whether physiological or intuitive, notice the feelings and information that appeared, and follow the breadcrumbs. Burrow through any roadblocks that may appear, and ignore all the stop signs. Keep writing until you feel like you've exhausted every avenue. Take your time and be patient with yourself as you work through this exercise. When you're finished, we'll be waiting for you in Chapter Three.

https://mysongcraft.com/members/

#3-Reach Down Deep

"I think we're creative all day long. We have to have an appointment to have that work out on the page. Because the creative part of us gets tired of waiting, or just gets tired."

Mary Oliver
Poet

Artist's Estate

"If only' I was sitting on the porch of that cabin on the edge of the river, with the snow-capped mountains looming off in the distance, my hot cup of coffee next to my Moleskine and freshly sharpened number two pencil, the trees stirring in the breeze, here for the next three days with nothing else to distract me, 'then' there would be nothing stopping me from writing every single day." How many 'if' and 'then' proclamations do we daily make as an excuse for not writing? Devoting time and energy in a consistent way to cultivate our creative process is critically important.

At first glance, this chapter may seem out of sequence, but it is both the beginning and endpoint of imagining a creative life for ourselves; it is about actualizing vision, of turning our "if only" into a "yes, really" and creating the physical, mental and inspirational space, with all the necessary implements at the ready so we can wholeheartedly delve into our art.

Realms of the Artist

When we think about a creative environment, there are actually three spatial components to consider: 1) physical, 2) mental, and 3) spiritual. Our physical space is the office, studio, or kitchen table, the place where we typically sit to really focus and press our work forward. The relationship between the songwriter and this space is important because it signals a shift in thinking that says, "Ok, I'm taking a break from the rest of my life, ready to roll up my sleeves and write." When we enter that space, we want to have a neat desk and an uncluttered mind, so mental space, trying to set aside worry and distraction, is crucial to the process as well. And, inasmuch as creativity is the expression of the heart and soul, it is crucial to clear a spiritual space which acknowledges the source of our inspiration - that which connects us to the creative realm where all things are possible.

Creating Physical Space

Nancy says: The mental preparation and mindset for the variety of jobs we are called upon to do throughout the day are unique to the task at hand. For me, the most important criteria in making the shift is having a clean, safe and inspired place to work, along with the right tools at the ready to get the job done. My creative work takes many forms; songwriting is only one of them. I have many commitments throughout the day so I want the mental shift to my songwriting practice to be as effortless as possible. Having tools, instruments, notepad and books, all hanging on the wall or on my desk where they are easily found and accessible, helps me prepare to get my work done.

Laura says: I am way more "lateral" than linear, and finding the balance between creative thinking and distraction is a tough one for me. While my songs are written wherever I find myself, on scraps of paper, on receipts, on my phone, I have a "songwriting central" place in my home, with access to a variety of instruments, a proper

*desk and writing tools. It is the place that holds me steady
for writing, honing, crafting. It's the "99% perspiration"
place. It is not about anything else, and it offers me the
clear choice to focus on writing.*

Perhaps the idea of having just one creative place to play
and write feels too limiting and suffocating to a free-spirit. And
unrealistic, given the busy lives we lead. We are not talking
about stifling the muse because as we know, inspiration can
strike at the oddest times - driving, in the shower, shopping for
groceries, when we are nowhere near that special room with
musical paraphernalia at our fingertips. We are suggesting that
we can create within ourselves a place in which we honor our
songwriting practice, and ourselves as creative beings; where
we intentionally set aside all else, and devote time and space
to work our craft. A space to dream, to think, to believe, to be
fearless and vulnerable, so we can dip our pens in the well of
abundance and sling our guts out to dry; a place to focus, free
from distraction, to ignite the spark of an idea and let it burn
away every self-imposed boundary until there is nothing left
but raw, beautiful emotion rising out of the ash and onto the
page. Such a space creates an environment that maximizes our
chances of success.

We think, "But all I really need is a notebook and guitar, and
I can write anywhere!" This is true. Some of us set up at a coffee
shop because we are restless, need a change of scenery and
can write and sip tea for hours. Some of us go for long drives
and let our minds wander like a winding back road. Having a
dedicated creative space, however, helps us to overcome those
nasty voices we discussed in chapter one which say, "I'm not
worthy," or "This isn't important."

Creating a space for songwriting encourages us to make a commitment to honoring our creative selves. Here are a few essential requirements for a creative environment:

1) Free from distraction: We have a conditioned response to that tiny little red dot that tells us that an email is waiting. Technology has us well trained. When we are in our creative space, we must turn everything off – the phone, Facebook, email. Put a "Do Not Disturb" sign on the door, and leave all worries on the doorstep. Be here now.

2) Dump the Excuses: As discussed in chapter two, being a creative person is a privilege which we must nurture. Make time and space for that creativity. If we continue to live with an attitude of "lack", then our "lack of results" will speak for itself.

3) Resources & Decor: Creative space is not just empty space. Having proper materials at hand is essential. Suggestions for items to have on hand are 2B pencils, a notebook, a laptop, a rhyming dictionary, instruments, a coffee pot, and reference materials. Good lighting is a must, and a sleeping dog or cat can help, too. Hang inspirational posters on the wall, awards and recognition, instruments, etc. Turn your studio into a 'curiosity cabinet' if you want to; with relics, modern art and shot glasses! Hang a nerf basketball net on the back of the door and fill shelves with your favorite books and music. Make it yours.

4) Morgue File: This term originally referred to the paper folders that investigators or reporters used to house notes and old articles for future reference. Designers, illustrators and teachers adopted this practice to collect ideas for projects or lessons. A shoebox, binder or a desk drawer will all serve as a morgue file. Songwriters are always collecting ideas, but storing them in a specific place is an intentional way to collect bits and pieces of inspiration that cross our path. Flipping or sorting through your file is a great way to get the creative juices flowing when your stuck. Our morgue files have napkin notes, post-its, pages torn from magazines, photographs, ticket stubs, old letters and even faded rose petals.

Mental Space

"The universe buries strange jewels deep within us all, and then stands back to see if we can find them." - Elizabeth Gilbert, Big Magic: Creative Living Beyond Fear

Possibilities and ideas exist everywhere. We inhale and exhale them so routinely we often miss their magic and mystery. They fade into the great expanse of daily routine, and we stop noticing them. But like stars in our universe, they are there even when we are not paying attention. The probing Hubble Telescope is proving day after day that space is more vast than we can fathom, containing a multitude of stars and planets we never knew existed. Our imaginations are certainly big enough to sit in the Captain's chair on the USS Enterprise, pushing the boundaries of the familiar and encountering mysteries not yet conceived of, but we must train them to pay attention. Inspiration is all around us, often in the most unlikely of places - even here on earth!

Nancy says, "A short walk in the middle of a project is something I do when I'm stuck. I like to play the game of 'found objects'. It's amazing how a button, paperclip, rusty bolt or a piece of broken tail light can spark a new idea."

Laura says, " I swim several times a week, with a snorkel and goggles. In the water there is nothing to to distract me, not even figuring out when to breathe. My mind is free to go wherever it wants to go. Thoughts come up and if they intrigue me, I follow their thread. If not, I let them go.

Once we understand how we operate within the universal creative process, inspiration and discovery will be more fluid as well. So if you want better, more consistent creative results, try adding some of these mindful habits to your practice:

1. Have an active curiosity. Be interested in people, your surroundings, history and current events, how things are made, how things are broken. Observe the world with big questions: Who, what, where, why, when, how. Purposely seek out new opportunities and challenges. Intellectual curiosity and openness to emotions and fantasy will feed your creative genius. Learn a skill outside of your specialty. Try a new recipe, take the train, learn the names of trees and flowers, change the oil in your lawnmower. Say yes instead of no and follow the detours.

2. Take time for solitude and daydreaming. How will we ever hear our creative voice if we don't take time to reflect and listen to what it's saying? Time spent alone allows our minds to wander, which is a critical part of creative processing. When ideas show up out of the blue, it's usually because our minds were relaxed and off somewhere in la la land.

3. Don't be afraid to fail. Resilience is a huge part of success. Like a photographer who takes 100 shots to get the one perfect picture, songwriters are going to write some stinkers on the way to getting that Grammy winner. Or even the Granny-winner- that song that makes your Grandma cry every time she hears it.

4. Find the humor. Humor makes us playful and laughter eases our mood. Creativity has a horrible time breaking through solemnity or self-importance. So squelch the ego and go make a funny face in the mirror. Even the most serious work will benefit from a little light-heartedness.

5. Be Fearless and Honest. There may be times when the muse serves up ideas that are too big, too scary to take on. Hard as it may be, it's important to face them head on and tackle whatever part you can. Maybe you will take a run at the same idea several times, over a period of time, until you've reached the nugget of truth. Maybe you won't get there, but you sure won't get there if you don't try. Not every song ever written has to be recorded, let alone performed. It's ok to leave plenty of film on the cutting room floor. It's more important to do the work even if every creation isn't an oscar contender.

Space for Spirituality

Spirituality is about being aware there is a 'bigger picture', a higher power, a muse, an energy source - call it what you like, but it is believing we all exist together as part of something amazing and awesome. Stand on the shore and stare out at the ocean and you'll feel it. Look up at a clear night sky when the milky way is thick and brilliant and you'll feel it there too. On the mezzanine atop the Eiffel Tower, looking over the city of Paris, connecting with the history, the vibrance, the clutter, the charm, and it's there too! Sitting under a tree in the park listening to the laughter of children running through water spouts, or holding a bedside vigil with a dying parent, you feel the connection. It is a beautiful and necessary part of our creative practice to 'be still'; to allow ourselves to experience moments of transcendence and awe.

1. Be aware of the beauty that surrounds you. 'Jazz-like' architecture of Frank Gehry, the New York Botanical Garden in The Bronx, the Grand Canyon; art and beauty are essential to the creative spirit, wherever you may find it. It's like holding up a lens and seeing a reflection of the divine. Beauty takes us to another plain - higher, lower, wider, narrower - and perhaps most importantly, to a truer and more whole experience of who we are.

> *Nancy says, "Years ago I visited an exhibit of painters at the Guggenheim in NYC. As I circled the room I was in awe, relishing the brush strokes, the use of light and dark, and analysing subtleties of these famous compositions. Then in one surprising moment I found myself standing in front of Van Gogh's Sunflowers; I literally and simply gasped, and tears streamed down my cheeks. I'm still not sure I can articulate why I was so moved by this painting and not the others, but most definitely, it was a soul encounter."*

> *Laura says, "I was on a run through the woods when I*

came upon a budding oak tree, covered with tender bright green leaves. As I got closer, I realized that in that same tree, was a flock of about 30 goldfinches, and then, a single bluebird. It stopped me dead in my tracks. The green, yellow and spot of blue against the bright fluffy white clouded sky was simply breathtaking. And only given to me because I had my head up, looking."

Aesthetic experience connects us to inspiration at the source. Of course not everything needs to be sophisticated to be beautiful; listen to the coo of mourning doves, wisp with the clouds and sway with jack pines, lose yourself in a peepers concerto, or catch a flake of snow on the palm of your hand. Incredible beauty lives in the simple and ordinary moments between sleep and awake. So whether it's beautifully woven bed sheets, an arrangement of tulips on the mantle or the ballet of leaves in the rain, surround yourself with beauty, but more important, go looking for it.

2. Find your flow. The 'flow', also known as "being in the zone", refers to the energizing focus and complete enjoyment in the process of an activity. You know you've entered the flow when you finally look up at the clock and hours have passed by without having any real consciousness of time. Flow is also associated with immense joy and satisfaction. There's been a lot of research around flow, and though it's not fully understood, being engaged in an activity that is challenging and arouses passion are its two key components. So pick up your pencil, your paint, your canvas - whatever gets your mojo going - and get to work!

3. Practice mindfulness. Meditate, slow down, breathe. When we're in the 'flow' we are already immersed in 'creative mindfulness' which means we are creating with abandon and joy. But for the times we are not engaged in our process, when a herd of self-doubt comes galloping through the studio, kicking up fear and insecurity, a mindfulness practice will tame the mustangs and help the dust settle. This practice is also widely known to reduce stress, improve focus and boost mental clarity. Nancy uses Andy Puddicomb's app "Headspace" for daily guided meditation, and it is an excellent place to learn how to integrate meditation into your life. Laura is lucky enough to have a Buddhist monastery in her town and has taken many classes there in meditation. There are many healing centers, websites and books about meditation just waiting for you. Or if you prefer a more unstructured approach, try sitting in a comfortable position for 10 minutes and focus on your breath, just breathing in, breathing out. When thoughts or worries pop into your head (and they will!), try to just let them go, like troublesome balloons that impede your view. Give it a try!

Creative Practice: Three Things A Day

Here is a powerful yet simple method to integrate a mindful creative practice in your daily life.

1. Look for inspiration every day. Use your curiosity to invite something amazing and new into your daily view. In other words, open your mind to the diverse sensory stimuli surrounding you and use it as a doorway to inspiration. Sight, sound, smell, taste, and touch inform our brains about our environments so routinely that it's easy to overlook their awesomeness. So use your head and your heart as you get reacquainted with these five magnificent gifts, and find fresh insight every single day.

2. Document your findings. Next, spend a few minutes documenting your discovery. Write or sketch in your journal, take a photograph or make a voice recording. Look for unique and distinguishing features in your observations. Explain why this particular 'thing' was inspiring. Documentation is incredibly valuable because it helps us to 'remember' the emotion of the moment. It allows us the opportunity to savor it's flavor a second time. Often, when we find new inspiration, we connect dots to other fabulous ideas, so jot them down before they fly away!

3. Share in a meaningful way. "What the world needs now, is love sweet love" is a lyric from a fabulous song penned by Burt Bacharach and Hal David. Let's rewrite it just a bit: "What the world needs now, is you, sweet you"! That's right, YOU! Society at large is obsessed with measuring ability and talent, and comparing performance and earnings, but it is done to the detriment of the human spirit. When we share our inspiration, we offer meaningful connection and invite people to tune into their own aspirations for fuller awareness in their lives. Blog, share your photos, be a guest speaker, or simply have a conversation with your family at the dinner table.

We strongly encourage you to cultivate a daily creativity practice in your life and hope you'll share your findings with us on social media. Use the hashtag ***#mycreativeheart*** to connect with our growing community.

https://mysongcraft.com/members/

#4-Artist's Estate

"There is nothing to writing. All you do is sit down at a typewriter and bleed."

Ernest Hemingway
American journalist, novelist, and short-story writer.

Focus Your Lens

We hope that the concept of the Artist's Estate is helpful to you in pursuing your creative practice, and trust you've gathered valuable information in the writing exercises of previous chapters. Hopefully you've found a trail of breadcrumbs to lead you to a new lyric. Actually, chances are there is more than one direction you could follow in your notes to create a song. It's important to give yourself permission to use only the material that best serves one central theme, so be fearless. Sometimes it may require leaving your favourite line behind. Weaving more than one theme will distract and confuse the listener. It's ok to leave out factual details if they don't serve the emotional context of the song. Our goal is to advance the narrative. Stay on the path and avoid unnecessary detours, because not all roads lead to the finish line.

Nancy says, I was intrigued by a story that was set at the turn of the last century in a small farming community near my home. A young mother and her baby died during the birthing of twin boys. They were buried together in the church graveyard. A week later, the second baby died, and when they returned to bury him, they found a single white glove laying on the ground beside the grave. Inside the coffin, only the clothes of the mother remained. The grave had been robbed! Her husband found and retrieved his wife's body from a university medical lab, and he brought her home and lay her in the ground a second time. It took me a long time to start writing this song because I couldn't figure out how to fit all the elements into three minutes. I really needed to filter through the details to decide what would be useful to the story. In the end, the husband's character became most important to me, and I wrote the song from his perspective. I ignored the white glove. I also decided it would be more efficient to have the mother give birth to just one baby. When I focused on Ben's grief and shock at the atrocities, the song almost wrote itself. While I was making these decisions I kept hearing the voice of songwriting professor Pat Pattison saying, "It doesn't have to be factually true to be emotionally true." Good lesson.

So where do we go from here? In this chapter, we will build upon the stream writing and mapping exercises to further construct the framework for a lyric. Let's get to work.

Find the Gems

Let's go back to the streaming exercises you did in Chapter Two and look over what you wrote. What struck a nerve? Perhaps it was a feeling that was difficult to face. Or maybe an emotional memory that spawned new self-awareness. It might have been hilarious, but whatever the case, take a deep breath, and explore the feelings and circumstances even further. Once you know the 'what', ask 'why' is this 'the thing' that stands out? Look for clarity in the details and emotions as they surface, and make note of them.

Next, look through your notes and circle or underline any words, phrases or thoughts that resonate, sound interesting, or strike a unique chord. Transcribe those lines to a new page. Try to find a connection, a thread that ties any of the words or phrases together. Review your Object Map. Is there an underlying tone offering direction for comparison between your objects? Explore, experiment and begin to lay out the canvas.

Nancy's Gems:

If I had cut down those maples
And stacked the wood by the shed
Would it have been enough
To keep warm until winter's end
The blame that you shoulder
Is not yours alone
So i'll share your sorrow
Row by row
It takes a lot of lumber
The lumber and a hammer
But every blow
Troubles drowned and buried
In the morning reappear

Laura's Gems:

Paradise
* through a six-year old's eyes*
Comics, pinball, ice cream and more

Delights in my Gramma's candy store
Newspapers in before daylight
She closed up shop close to midnight
Relentless, day after same kind of day
Trampled her spirit, wore it away
Counted out change while the hours stood still
But rang out, rang up on the old metal till
Lining up for news and smokes
Same faithful customers, same tired jokes
Seemed like it ought to have been a good life
But she longed for something else
The broken down cardboard boxes were tied up with twine
She was tied down by debt and by time

Take it to the Next Level

"Songwriting is a bitch. And then it has puppies" Steven Tyler

Now, build upon your lines. It is not necessary to worry about meter or rhyme just yet, but do not push away inspiration if the lines flow out in song form. When the words on the page ring true to the heart, follow that trail. Remember you don't have to tell the whole story, just a story. When writing a song about someone's storybook romance, you don't necessarily have to include the part about the messy ugly divorce three years later. Hone in on the part of the story that is most intriguing or evocative. To tell a story that is engaging and believable, it is important to create a scenario that rings true to the core. If it does, then someone similarly situated should be able to "step into" the experience too. It is important to express ideas in a way that invites participation. Remember the "tell me vs. show me" examples from Chapter Two. Start with the kernel of a personal truth and then make it accessible for everyone with language that rolls the film.

Laura says: In the aftermath of Hurricane Katrina, there was a "flood" of media coverage. I was caught by a photograph of a young girl in the foreground, maybe age 14 or 15, in a party dress. Behind her, in a soft, out-of-focus blur, were a few others, with guitars, a bass, a fiddle. The girl had her eyes closed and this beatific smile on her face. And I thought 'Wow, what do you do if you're a teenage girl, with all of the drama that goes along with teenage girlhood, and some other, huge drama comes along to eclipse your own?' I gave that girl a name, imagined what that story could be, and wrote her song from just seeing that photo.

"She was only 15 when she had to quit school
Her family needed her pay
Ever since the day the flood waters came
And washed her hope and her childhood away" -

"Rosie" ©2007 Laura E Zucker

Nancy's Next Level

I really wish things had been different for my Uncle. As I sketched out these lines, I could see my heart open and ache for him and others with similar addictions. I was too

*young to be the advocate he needed, but that didn't stop
me from feeling his pain. I couldn't help. But I wanted to.*

*If I had saved the wood of those two maples
Cut and stacked them beside the shed
I could have offered you their warmth
When the cold winter wouldn't end
The blame you had to shoulder
Was not yours alone to bear
But logs left to snow and rain
Will rot and disappear*

> *The world has its sorrows
> Build and repair
> So what can't be solved
> With a six pack of beer*

*It takes a lot of lumber
To frame all four walls
Check them with a level
So the building doesn't fall
Every blow of the hammer
Hits squarely in the heart
Troubles bleed like slivers
And again the thirst starts*

> *The world has its sorrows
> Build and repair
> So what can't be solved
> With a six pack of beer*

Laura's Next Level

Laura says: "As I started to write from the map I'd done, and especially as I made the connections and refined the lyrics, I realized that now, as an adult myself, I had an entirely new appreciation for my grandmother and the life that she led. It came as a complete shock to me.

Paradise
Through a six-year old's eyes
Comics, pinball, ice cream and more
In my Gramma's candy store
Newspapers came in before daylight
She closed up shop close to midnight
Tending the line-up for news and for smokes
Same faithful customers, same tired jokes
She worked hard and mostly she stayed to herself
But oh, how she longed for something else
The broken down boxes were tied up with twine
She was tied down by duty and time.

Taking Form

But, you ask - how can I write this song if I don't know how to write a song? There are myriad ways to structure songs, and we will explore some of the essentials to get you going.

If you've been doing the exercises in the previous chapters, you will have a pretty good idea of your central theme, collected some gems and brought them to the next level. Now it's time to think of them in terms of verses and chorus, and possibly a bridge and/or pre chorus. Let's define each of these:

Verse: Lays out the details of your story and sets the tone of your theme.

Chorus: The main point of the song. This is the part you want repeated over and over. Musically, it is the resting place for the listeners' ear. The chorus is also referred to as "the hook", the idea or phrase that you think is most likely to appeal to your audience, the takeaway of your song.

Bridge: What's left to say? A bridge is a unique place to add an overarching explanation of the song, or an underpinning, not necessarily part of the main story line, but adds substance to or imbues with extra meaning what you've written in the verses and chorus.

Pre-Chorus: Comes after a verse with a distinct melody, and typically short, like one or two lines. It's purpose is to build up to the Chorus and often repeats the same lyrics.

We can create *verse, pre-chorus, chorus* and *bridge* in various combinations, but not all of these elements are necessary in every song. Let's call this the 'overall structure', where the letter "V" is a verse, "C" is the chorus, "**Br**" is the bridge, and "**Pr**" is a pre-chorus. Here are a few scenarios: The Beatles song "*Get Back*" is written **V C V C**. as is Garth Brooks "*I Got Friends in Low Places*". The Beatles song "*She Loves You*" is **C V V C V C**, starting with a chorus rather than a verse. A typical commercial country song is often written like this: **V C V C Br C**, like Miranda

Lambert's hit song *"The House That Built Me"* written by Allen Shamblin and Tom Douglas. Greenday's *"Boulevard of Broken Dreams"* is **V V C Br In** (where 'In' is a vocal/instrumental "ah, ah" section), and then the structure is repeated again. Once you know what your song form/structure is going to be, it must be consistent so your listener will understand where you're going next. Writing with a "roadmap" in mind allows you to have a clear path and gives your audience a feeling of familiarity with your song right from the start.

Taking another look at Nancy's 'next level' above, it seems like she's going to follow V C V C. Laura's next level isn't quite as developed yet, and that's ok. We'll see where it goes in the next section.

Polish the Gems

Once a verse or two or three are written, reflect on the questions below to clarify the message of the lyric even further and continue to develop your cogent theme and resonant truths.

1) What am I trying to say?

2) What have I already said?

3) What does that leave?

Take everything already done, boil it down, then wring it out for a second round of clarifying, simplifying. Once the central thoughts are written down, remove unnecessary details, asking,

"Does this detail serve the central image or idea of the song, or is it distracting?"

It's also time to consider meter and rhyme, as well as the structure of each verse and chorus, and bridge and pre-chorus if you want to use them. What do we mean by meter? Remember in high school english class when you read Shakespeare and talked about "iambic pentameter" and couplets? This is the same thing: meter refers to the stresses on the syllables of the words in each line, the number of syllables in each line, and the number of lines in a verse / chorus / bridge / etc. Meter is created by controlling the accented and non-accented syllables. They create a rhythm and a flow, in a grouping dictated by the time signature of your song which is often in groups of three or four. For instance, *"Ladybug, ladybug, where have you been?"* which corresponds to three beats per measure. *"Mary had a little lamb. It's fleece was white as snow,"* illustrates a four beat per measure pattern.

Meter also refers to the number of lines you have in a particular section. This will be determined by what you're trying to say, and also by the emotion you're trying to convey. The song "Don't Worry Be Happy" (Bobby McFerrin) has an even six lines in each verse. It makes the song feel resolved and happy.

"Here's a little song I wrote
You might want to sing it note for note
Don't worry, be happy
In every life we have some trouble
But when you worry you make it double
Don't worry, be happy" -

Don't Worry, Be Happy © 1988 Bobby McFerrin

On the other hand, an odd number of lines can make a song feel unsettled, like Alanis Morrisette does in the five-lined chorus of "*You Oughta Know*".

"And I'm here, to remind you
Of the mess you left when you went away
It's not fair, to deny me
Of the cross I bear that you gave to me
You, you, you oughta know"

You Ought to Know, © 1995 Alanis Morissette

Also note the uneven number of syllables in each line, and how it enhances the chaotic, angry feel of the lyric. Seven syllables in lines 1, 3 and 5, and 10 in lines 2 and 4. The meter is consistent both in count and the beat on which it is stressed. For instance, the words 'remind' and 'deny' both have stronger emphasis on the "-mind" and "-ny".

So remember, after you've worked so hard to 'Reach Down Deep' to connect with your emotional vulnerability, it is important to consider what effect meter will have on successfully conveying your message. Keeping meter consistent from verse to verse is a best practice.

Next up is rhyme, which has a structure all its own. There are different types of rhyme, and they can occur in various parts of your lyric. End rhyme is what occurs at (you guessed it!) the end of each line, like this:

"Here's a little song I wrote
You might want to sing it note for note".

Internal rhyme occurs within a line of your lyric. The sound repetition due to internal rhyme makes a lyric or story feel unified. It is employed to heighten the lyric's' effects, and this internal rhyme can take place in the same line or two separate alternating lines. Consider this James Taylor verse from "Sweet Baby James":

"There is a young cowboy, he lives on the range
*His horse and his **cattle** are his only companions*
*He works in the **saddle** and sleeps in the canyons*
Waiting for summer, his pastures to change"

  Sweet Baby James © 1970 James Taylor

Most often, you will hear of rhyme schemes being described as a function of their end rhymes, with rhyming words being given the same descriptor letter. For instance, the James Taylor lyrics below would be described as an **A B B A** rhyme scheme

*"There is a young cowboy, he lives on the **range [A]***
*His horse and his **cattle** are his only **companions [B]***
*He works in the **saddle** and sleeps in the **canyons [B]***
*Waiting for summer, his pastures to **change" [A]***

A very commonly used rhyme scheme is the **A B A B**, as employed here by the wonderful Texas singer-songwriter Brian Kalinec in his song "*The Fence*": (Notice how effectively he uses internal rhyme throughout this verse as well).

"Like raindrops sifting slowly through the window **screen**
A
*The minutes drip their torture on this august after***noon** **B**
*My fingers flip the moisture off the canvas of my can***teen**
A
Though i wipe my brow the sweat returns too **soon**" **B**

"The Fence" © 2012 Brian J Kalinec

Here are a couple of other rhyme scheme examples:

These times are hard **A**
And it's harder to heal **B**
When where you were born **C**
Decides what you fear **B**

It's time to be a brother **A**
Not my father's son **B**
I was born to be a bigot **C**
But that don't mean that I am one **B**

"Scars We Keep" © 2016 Crystal Hariu-Damore & Pete Damore

"I'd rather be a sparrow than a snail **A**
Yes I would **B**
If I could **B**
I surely would **B**
I'd rather be a hammer than a nail **A**
Yes I would **B**
If I could **B**
I surely would" **B**

"El Condor Pasa" © 1970 Paul Simon

Most of the examples above all use what's known as *"perfect rhyme,"* rhyme in which different consonants are followed by identical vowel and consonant sounds, such as in moon and June. Then there is *"near"* or *"slant"* or *"imperfect"* rhyme, which is characterized by stressed vowel sound in both words that are identical, as well as any subsequent sounds.

For example, imperfect rhymes could be: *amble, ample, angles, apple, apples, campus, candle, candles, chances, channels, classes, couples, fragile, gamble, hamlet, handle, handles, mammal, mantel, mantle, mantles, pampers, ramble, sample, sandals, scandal, shambles, strangles.* You get the idea.

There's no rule for what you should do in your songs, but it's always good to know "the rules" so you can make a conscious decision whether or not to break them. Beware: perfect rhyming carries with it the danger of forced rhymes, where it's obvious that the word was chosen primarily for the rhyme instead of the meaning. Good rhymes take time. So be prepared to write and rewrite – a lot – in order to get something that works really well. Opt for near rhyming when an exact rhyme isn't forthcoming. A near rhyme is often every bit as good as an perfect one, with the added benefit of likely being closer to what you really want to say. Often, near rhymes keep your listener more intrigued, as the lyrics are less predictable. If your meaning is strong and message is consistent, you may choose not to rhyme at all. The most important things is that your lyric offers a sense of internal pulse and rhythm.

Here is a great example of a song that climbed the charts and uses near rhyme to get its point across.

*"Hold the door say please say thank you **A***
*Don't steal, don't cheat, and don't lie **B***
*I know you got mountains to climb but **B***
*Always stay humble and kind **B***

*When the dreams you're dreamin' come to you **A***
*When the work you put in is realized **B***
*Let yourself feel the pride but **B***
*Always stay humble and kind" **B***

 "Humble and Kind" © 2016 Lori McKenna

So time to get back to work on your songs. Lose unnecessary words, tighten up the meter, ensure the images and metaphors in the song are working together, check your rhymes (or non-rhymes). Some words, some phrases may have to go to the editing room floor, and that is ok! Each and every word must serve the point of the song.

Editing isn't always easy, especially when your song comes from a raw, emotional place. Let's follow the life of Nancy's song *"Honestly"*. In a nutshell, it illustrates the choices to be made while constructing a song.

Nancy says, Years ago, when I was going through a difficult time in my relationship and grieving the loss of my church community, I sat with my journal and did some stream writing to poke around at the emotions I was feeling at the time, and then created a map. Here is a transcript of my initial writing:

"Honestly, I thought you'd already gone
I can't shake the feeling of watching you leave
And can't do a thing, can't even sing
Holding a photograph of earlier times
When were you ever mine?
No one offers advice, only judgment
Hindsight is easier truth,
The mirror behind the façade"

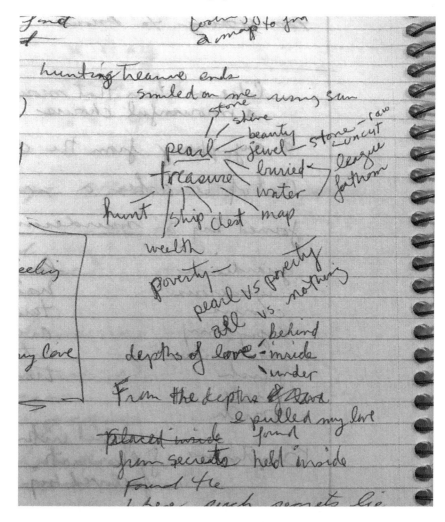

Some of this makes no sense at all, but there were a couple of lines that resonated with me and opened the door to more exploration. The lines I circled from this exercise were these: "Honestly, I thought you'd already gone, I can't shake the feeling of watching you leave," and "When were you ever mine?"

Taking this to the next stage, I decided to use the word 'treasure' as a metaphor for the missing pieces of my situation – perhaps with the idea that the universe had a secret map with directions to fix my problems. The following image is a shot from my notebook showing how I simply mapped out the word 'treasure'. The idea of a rare pearl struck a chord, so my first verse draft builds on this Notion.

> "Honestly, I thought you had already gone
> I can't shake this awful feeling of moving on
> Were you ever really mine?
> Or just a pearl to find / A rare pearl to find
> From the depths I pulled my love
> From secrets held inside"

At this point, I was ready to polish the verse, both lyrically and melodically. The rhyme scheme fell into place using the form AABBCB, uneven, which served the emotion of this song. Typically, I will have fleshed out some sort of melody either in my head or on guitar at this stage. I'll pace around my room singing the words out loud, revisiting my notebook, editing and refining each and every line until it 'feels' right. The final version of verse one:

"Honestly, I thought you had already gone
I can't stand this awful feeling of moving on
Were you ever really mine?
Beautiful pearl to find
From the deep I pulled my love
Where such secrets lie"

"Honestly" © *2007 Nancy Beaudette*

A Note About Melody

Melody is an integral part of the songwriting process and helps facilitate the mood and emotion of the stories we tell. Melody frames the temperament of a song before we even start singing the lyrics. While this book is mainly about the words we write, we would be remiss not to talk about the marriage between the two. If the melody comes before the words start flowing, we must ask ourselves the same questions we posed earlier: Does it serve the song? Is it a distraction?

Mindful choices when selecting melody, key and tempo are critical in developing and communicating a story. For example, stories about death may not be well understood when delivered as polkas. On the other hand, "Bye Bye Blackbird", a story about facing failure, is much more palatable as a lighter moderate up-tempo.

Pack up all my cares and woe
Here I go feeling low
Bye-bye Blackbird
No one here can love or understand me

Oh, what hard luck stories they all hand me
Make my bed and light the light
I'll arrive late tonight
Blackbird bye-bye

"Bye Bye Blackbird" © 1926 Ray Henderson, Mort Dixon

Some may argue that this is actually a song about how nice it is to have a nest to return to. It is all about how a story is told. Ray Henderson and Mort Dixon knew what they meant, but expressed it in a way that invites not one, but two populations of listeners in, depending on their interpretation, and either way it is heard, it is easy to relate and step into.

What we're talking about is called *'prosody'*. In songwriting it refers to the way the writer sets the lyric to music; how the music matches the content of the song. Don Henley says *"Sometimes songwriters get a melody in their head and the notes will take precedence, so that they wind up forcing a word onto a melody. It doesn't ring true."* The interplay between melody and lyric should appropriately capture the emotion of the song by placing syllables and beats together at just the right places, so what is being said, and how it is being said, match up. Like making the word "low" occur on a low note in the melody, or stopping the music entirely on the word "stop" (think The Supremes' " *Stop In The Name Of Love*") The goal is for the music and lyrics to evoke the same emotion. Berklee Songwriting Professor Susan Cattaneo says, it *"is a critical element for a song to be successful...and it should be one of the first things you examine once you've finished your first draft."* Our choice of key and tempo are huge considerations as well. A happy song may be best served in a major key with an upbeat tempo, while a sad song may want to reside in a minor key and be played slower. Also watch for words like up, down, swing, move, roll, etc. These are opportunities for us to raise or lower our pitch, draw out a long note, or sing a phrase faster. All these nuances will lead to a long and happy union, so make every word and note serve the same purpose: the song.

"*I Will Always Love You*" written by Dolly Parton is a great example of prosody. This song was a chart topper before Whitney Houston's version became one of the best selling singles of all time. A song about separation and sorrow delivered with exceptional sentiment, soaring melody and musicality. U2's song "*Still haven't found what I'm looking for*" has angst in both melody and lyric as it pulls us straight into the longing and loneliness of life and our need to make everything make sense. What do these songs have in common? The emotional content of the lyric weaves its way into each note and rest in the song.

How Much or How Little to Say

Emily Saliers (one half of the Indigo Girls) wrote a song about Virginia Woolfe without ever once mentioning her name. It is less a description of Woolfe's life and more about Emily's relationship to Woolfe's writing. How does she start this story?

> "*The Mississippi's Mighty*
> *It starts in Minnesota*
> *At a place that you could walk across with 5 steps down.*"

Then she proceeds to explain the "*rush*" of emotion she felt when reading Wolfe's writing. "*At this point you rush right through me and I start to drown."* A mighty metaphor is born: an incipient river beginning with a trickle, a *"pinprick to my heart"* becoming an emotional obsession. We are invited into this song by the intrigue of the description of the Mississippi river. Where is this going? And then we are drawn into the scenario because we too have felt the passionate desire Emily describes, the sudden surge, the relentless power, the inescapable current of love when it takes hold. What a great story, beautifully told in an unexpected way.

"Before He Cheats", cleverly written by two men, is a 'woman scorned' song, but not just any ordinary woman scorned song. Chris Tompkins and Josh Kear set this song up to create an entire world that we get instantly: its values, its expectations and the morals of the players, with backhanded precision. *"Right now, he's probably buying her some fruity little drink 'cause she can't shoot whiskey."* We not only understand the actions described, but they're set in a context that instantly explains far more.

Some stories are written as purges of the writer's psyche and can potentially alienate listeners. A blatant story of naked pain may be too difficult for a general audience because it requires them to dip into their own well of pain. We have a choice about which kind of story we want to tell – one that is a writer's purge or one that tenderly invites a listener to dip in a toe and come closer to processing their own pain.

Nancy says, I once had a studio client who wanted to record fifteen songs about the horrendous sexual abuse she experienced as a young teen. I suggested reworking a number of them, not to alter her experience, but rather to create vignettes that would not alienate or scare her au-

dience and give them a variety of reasons to connect with her story. In the end, she decided to keep the songs exactly how they fell onto the page.

Bleeding on the page is optimal, digging down to excavate the emotion around each and every idea. But then it's our job as songwriters to sort through what we discover, find the metaphors and develop the language to support it without decimating the listener. But, if your intention is deeply personal and private, it's completely okay to write and file it under "therapeutic writing". And it's also absolutely your prerogative to perform these songs, being mindful of the risks that you take with your audience.

Take A Break

When we quit working on a song for a while, and even try to forget it, our subconscious mind is still going - combining, colliding and making associations in the background. Relaxation and play time are critical to the creative process as are mundane tasks, because they allow our songwriter brain the space to grow our ideas. When we're working on a new song, the melody and lyric stay with us all day, all week or all month long! We need to allow time for a line to stew and simmer, to assess its flavor and see how it's going to taste with the rest of the lyric we are writing. If we're shopping, weeding the garden, driving somewhere, our creative mind, consciously or subconsciously, is running through the recipe looking for the perfect herb to add next.

Nancy says, "I had been working on a song about two sisters from Ireland who were forced to leave the country during the famine in 1847. Their names were included on the manifest of a ship that had docked in my hometown of Cornwall, Ontario. The manifest listed Rose as deceased. Mary survived. I was able to construct a story about the women's voyage which went fairly smoothly until I got to the last verse. It needed a "Why should I care?" wrap up. It took over a month of rewriting and polishing to finally bring the song to the finish line. In my heart, I knew I wanted to address the calamities of mass emigration and history repeating itself despite our promises of "never again". If I tried to make a huge political statement I might overshadow the story of Mary and Rose. It had to be a balance, so finding the right words and sentiment were important. Literally, while I was 'sleeping on it', the word "season" entered my consciousness and fed me the closing lines the song needed.

*"So many summers have passed since that day
And still I lament o'er dear Rose's grave
The memory of her only mine to recall
But the weight of that season belongs to us all"*

"Mary And Rose" © 2018 Nancy Beaudette

So take a break. Go for a drive, have a cat nap (or nip), soak in the tub or stroll through the neighborhood. Let your subconscious do the heavy lifting for a while.

Writing Exercise: Fine Tooth Comb

By this point, we hope you've got the framework for a verse or two and a chorus. Using the tips discussed in this chapter, refine your lyric. Stay focused on a central idea and work the 'craft'. Remember, this is important work that we're doing. Our efforts matter and make a difference in the world. Comb through every line to make sure the story unfolds naturally.

Note the point of view. When we talk about ourselves, our opinions, and the things that happen to us, we generally speak in the first person. The biggest clue that a sentence is written in the first person is the use of first-person pronouns. Singular first-person pronouns include I, me, my, mine and myself. We, us, our, and ourselves are all plural first-person pronouns. The second-person point of view belongs to the person (or people) being addressed. This is the "you" perspective. Once again, the biggest indicator of the second person is the use of second-person pronouns: you, your, yours, yourself, yourselves. The third-person point of view belongs to the person (or people) being talked about. The third-person pronouns include he, him, his, himself, she, her, hers, herself, it, its, itself, they, them, their, theirs, and themselves. In third person songs, a narrator describes what the characters do and what happens to them. You don't see directly through a character's eyes as you do in a first-person narrative, but often the narrator describes the main character's thoughts and feelings about what's going on. Most of the time when people speak about themselves, they speak in the first person.

Make sure the voice is consistent, unless there is a compelling reason to change voices. A song that starts with "I did, I thought" probably shouldn't end with a "he did, she thought." That would be very confusing, unless you are actually writing about yourself and then other people as central to your story, or you've written a duet which requires different voices

Assess the timeline. Does the song have a linear narrative: beginning, middle, end? Think of each verse and chorus like a play in several acts. First verse and chorus introduce the story, verse two reveals more detail, and the bridge adds meaning or underpinning, and could be the place for things you really need to say that don't logically fit into the verse or the chorus. Most songs will end on a chorus, the place of familiarity you've created for your audience

Look out for 'filler' lines. These may be lines that repeat a detail you've already said in a slightly different way, or a line that is simply not relevant to the story. You may be tempted add a line mostly to get the rhyme, but don't settle. Remember, every lyric should advance the narrative.

Review your meter and rhyme. Say or sing the words out loud and listen to where the emphasized syllables land. The addition of a word or two may be necessary to meet the meter and melody of your song. Likewise, if a line feels crammed or clumsy try removing excess words or rearrange the phrase until it rolls off the tongue. Try to use natural language. Try to have the accents fall on the correct syllable of the words. Prepositions are a good place to start editing, as shown in the example below.

As the sun rises in the morning
Let's seize the day
There are only a few hours to play
And my youthful heart is yearning

Now remove the prepositions:

Sun rises in the morning
Seize the day
Only a few hours to play
My youthful heart is yearning

This gives the lyric more space, and it does not lose any of its intended meaning.

Nancy's polishing the gems progress

Nancy says, "It wasn't until I sketched out ideas for a second verse that I realized it was actually my first verse. It sets the song stage using carpentry as a metaphor for a sense of place and circumstance, and slowly reveals the angst of the blue collar man living with emotional pain. I really liked the first four lines in my draft but I'm choosing to leave those behind so I can focus more on my subject and less on me - i.e. what I would like to have done to help the man vs a more observational motif, written in the third person."

(Verse 1)
Sort and lay the lumber
Frame out all the walls
Check them with a level
And brace so they don't fall
Slivers of youth come knocking
Hit squarely in the heart
Every blow of the hammer
The thirst comes on hard

(Chorus)
A man has many sorrows
Some cannot be repaired
They just get nailed together
With a six pack of beer

(Verse 2)
He had a woman once
It didn't last for long
Fists curled in anger
Go off like a bomb
Better just to be alone
With tools of the trade
Two by fours and rafters
To hammer out his rage (repeat chorus)

(Bridge)
I wish I knew him better
Maybe sit and have a pint
Just to listen for a while
Hear what's on his mind (repeat chorus)

Laura's polishing the gems progress

Laura says, I spent a lot of time thinking about how ironic it was that in a place of brightly colored candy wrappers, soda fountain and comic books, a bright spirit could be crushed. I thought that my chorus would be about that. But in the end, what emerged for me was how good-natured and resilient my grandmother was, as she saved every penny to make their "escape" from that gruelling life, never becoming embittered.

(Verse 1)
Paradise
Through a six-year old's eyes
Comics, pinball, ice cream and more
In my Gramma's candy store
Newspapers came in before daylight
She closed up shop close to midnight

(Chorus)
She smiled, and she dreamed
On the tunes she hummed made her escape
Her own hopes a tiny tied bundle inside
Of the prison of day after day after day.

(Verse 2)
Tending the line-up for news and for smokes
Same faithful customers, same tired jokes
She worked hard and mostly she stayed to herself
But oh, how she longed for something else
The broken down boxes were tied up with twine
She was tied down by duty and time.

(Chorus)
And she smiled, and she dreamed
On the tunes she hummed made her escape
Her own hopes a tiny tied bundle inside
of the prison of day after day after day

(Bridge)
How bitter to live a life not of your own
No matter how sweet your wares

Now it's your turn. Go back to your notebook. Pick up your guitar, or go to your instrument of choice, and play your song with discerning ears. We're almost there.

https://mysongcraft.com/members/

#5-Focus Your Lens

"I've learned that people will

forget what you said, people will

forget what you did, but people

will never forget how you made

them feel."

Maya Angelou
*American poet, singer, memoirist, and
civil rights activist.*

Tell Your Story

When our work is done well, it can have a long-lasting effect on the people who care to listen. If we are lucky enough to have even an ounce of the notoriety of the aforementioned performers, we get glimpses of the impact our songs have on the people around us. In the previous chapters, we have calmed the critic enough to get something written; we have reached down deep to connect with something true; we have made space to create; we have communicated our nuggets in our best, most carefully crafted, most authentic voice. So, in this chapter, we will get into the nitty gritty honing our work through constructive criticism and audience feedback.

Presenting Your Song

Nancy says: When I was a teenager, I joined a church choir, and in relatively short time, became the choir director, a position I held for the next twenty-five years. It was the best training ground I could have asked for in preparation for a solo performance career all these years later. Upon reflection, I was so stiff and serious and nervous to be in front of people back then. One time, I entered a songwriting competition at a local fair. My friends all came out to support and cheer me on. When I took the stage and started playing, I literally forgot over half the words to my song. I was mortified, but the look on the faces of my friends, their wide eyes and overextended smiles, forced me to continue, making up lines and even finding rhymes throughout the performance. I'm sure my knees knocked the whole time, but I finished the song and even walked away with a first-place ribbon. My friends and family have always been a safe place for me to explore and share my creations, even when I was less than my best.

Laura says: I had the honor of being a Kerrville NewFolk finalist very early in my career. I had practiced my songs within an inch of their lives, and I was ready. I stood in the wings of the Threadgill Stage at the festival grounds. I had done some breathing backstage, came out onto the stage when I was introduced, and managed to give a cogent backstory intro to my song, but when I began to introduce it, I could not for the life of me remember what the name of the song was. I was mortified. But there I was, so I took a deep breath, and I told everyone that if they figured it out before I did, they could tell me. And you know what? Everyone laughed and clapped, and I could feel how much they wanted me to succeed, and the rest went off without a hitch.

Yes indeed folks, it happens to all of us. We forget the lines, play wrong chords, and don't even know the title of our songs sometimes. As much as we prepare, that black hole, otherwise known as 'stagefright', is a reality. Breathe - you can do this. Be thoroughly rehearsed. Have a lyric sheet or a tablet on hand, tune your instrument ahead of time and most importantly, try to be yourself. Share your work. Tell the story.

Where we choose to play will determine in some part, the type of feedback we receive. Early on in your career, it is a good idea to play in safe places where feedback tends to be encouraging and constructive. Home, school, church, temple, or to best friends on skype are all great places to try out new songs. Open mic nights are also ideal places to step out for the first time. The awkward yet exciting moment you show your baby to the world is best done with folks who understand the privilege and the courage to bare all.

Athletes study re-runs of games to learn from their errors and work to improve plays, and videos of our performance offer a treasure trove of information too. Sometimes we need to step away to be objective. Get out your smartphone, take a selfie video and listen to your song with new ears and eyes.

Attending songwriting workshops or engaging with a professional songwriting mentor are also highly recommended. These facilitators have been in the game for a long time and offer us invaluable experience. They hand out informed evaluations of our work, help us evolve and rise to our potential, and are a source of encouragement and inspiration when we get stumped.

Objective Listening

Remember this: all critique is subjective and is offered through the individual lens of the person delivering it. You don't have to change anything in your song if you don't want to, but if the advice is coming from a place of respect and expertise, you may want to mull it over. That being said, if the feedback received feels harsh and demeaning, the person giving the critique is probably not the right fit for you. Keep looking until you find a person or group that knows how to be supportive and challenging at the same time.

> *Laura says: I had a one-on-one songwriting critique with an "industry professional", who made a living offering songwriting classes. He told me that the only way my song would be effective was to take out an entire verse and rewrite the chorus in a way that simply eviscerated it. I was devastated and angry, and I vowed to ignore his advice. But as I thought about what he objected to in the song, I realized that I could address the objection by changing one word in the chorus, which I did, and I think it actually made it a more effective song. I guess my point is that even if you don't trust the motives of the one giving the critique, or don't agree with the advice as given, there is still room for reflection and change. We tend to cling to our songs, and letting go enough to re-write and edit is so so challenging, because you think you've already bared your heart and soul, and now you have to peel down yet another layer. To the very bone. That's where the truth often lives.*

Not all advice will be helpful, but all can be useful. Knowing how our songs reach an audience is priceless information. Did they follow the story or were they confused? Did they feel the emotion we wanted to convey? Were they distracted by some performance issue that kept them from focusing on the song?

Nancy says: I had an idea for a song after attending my first estate sale. I was quite moved by how this person's house felt so lived in, yet all these strangers were rifling through her belongings. During my walk through the house, it became apparent to me that someone in the home had recently passed away. It felt disrespectful to be there. The draft of my first verse went like this:

"Dishes in the sink
A cup of tea she didn't drink
The news on channel four
A pair of slippers by the door
Something tells me
She left in a hurry
Got the doctor on the phone
Said I think it's time to go
So, she waved her house goodbye
And was gone by supper time"

I played the song for someone whose opinion I respected, and she asked how I knew about the conversation with the doctor. Fact is, I didn't, I made it up. In the scheme of things, I couldn't have known that information. I had started writing from the perspective of the woman rather than my experience of the situation. I needed the lyric to be consistent one way or the other. I changed it to this:

"Dirty dishes in the sink
A cup of tea she didn't drink
Stack of mail on the floor
Pair of slippers by the door
Something tells me

She left in a hurry
The sign said everything must go
No offer is too low
Strangers rummage for a deal
As if she wasn't real"

> *"Something Tells Me", (C)2011 Nancy Beaudette*

The rewrite is more authentic because the song focused on my vantage point and sentiment. The other problem with that first draft was the rushed chain of events after getting that desperate news from the doctor. I don't know of anyone who was diagnosed with an illness one minute and sold the house a few hours later! Still, the setup and hook of the song, "Something tells me she left in a hurry," points to the realization that it all happened too fast – the loss unexpected and profound. It was grueling to rewrite the verse, but completely worth the effort in the long run.

One of the most difficult parts of songwriting is deciding if or when to rewrite. We tend to fall in love with our songs and get defensive when they are criticized. We blame the audience for not being perceptive enough. The truth is, if our audience is confused or misses what we were trying to convey, we haven't done our job well enough, and we should rewrite. It may take only the tweak of a word or two. It may take cutting a whole verse or writing a stronger bridge. We think of this as "distilling" the essential message. We have to boil down every verse, each phrase, and every single word until the only thing left is 99 proof.

Sometimes a particular cultural expression or poetic mysticism is exactly what we have intended to write, even if our audience fails to understand. Leonard Cohen, Bob Dylan, and many others have left us wondering about a song's meaning, so we can give ourselves permission to write in that style as well. That being said, we are not Leonard or Bob. Cryptic or ethereal writing only works if there's a door for the audience to walk through so they can be in the room with you. If it's clear your listeners aren't 'getting it' perhaps you need to open the door a little wider. Inevitably, you get to make the final decision about what to bottle or pour down the drain. Just be mindful of the connection you're trying to build with your audience.

So how do we really know if our audience is "getting it"? Listen to them. If someone says, "You sang exactly what I was feeling", you know you've achieved your goal. If there are tears during a touching song and laughter while singing a funny one, it's a sure sign you've done something right. An extended applause is telling as well. Also, when your song hits the mark people will want to share their own story with you. Nancy has a song about playing hockey out on the pond as a kid, and every single time she performs it, numerous audience members, usually men, will tell her of childhood exploits on their neighborhood rinks. Laura had a woman from the audience come up to her after a show and say that it was as if Laura had been reading her diary. We have achieved our songwriting goals when the lyrics we have written call forward emotions and experiences our listeners believe are unique to them.

It's time. Share your creation with someone: your spouse, a friend, or a group. Ask for feedback, starting with "what did you like about the song" to get a little positive reinforcement right off the bat. Ask if they were confused at any point during the song. Listen carefully to the answers. Resist the temptation to 'defend' an idea or a line. Just contemplate the comments shared, take them back to your studio and hold them up against your work to see if they're justified.

Exercise: Refine and Shine

Refine: improve (something) by making small changes, in particular make (an idea, theory, or method) more subtle and accurate.

When will the song be finished? We wish we could answer that, but ultimately, you will know. The more experience you have as a songwriter, the better you will get at discerning a song's completion. For Nancy, the song is officially 'done' when it's been recorded. Until that point, tweaking is allowed. Laura has several songs that have been changed even after they were recorded, because they have evolved a little bit further and she found a line that worked better than the original.

So let's take another look at our lyric and see if there are any stumbling blocks or closed doors. Spit, polish, refine, re-peat.

Nancy's Refined Lyric

Nancy says, "I ended up crafting several drafts before accepting this as my final version. The melody is fairly simple, mostly just three chords (there's a minor in the

*bridge) and a spacious, mid-tempo oldtime vibe. Singing
the song aloud, over and over again helps me hear what's
working or what needs fixing. I fuss with every single
word until it just feels and sounds right in my heart and
head.*

(Verse)
Sort out the lumber
Frame up the walls
Check 'em with a level
Brace so they don't fall
Every blow of the hammer
Hit square to the heart
Can't pull out the sliver
Thirst comes on hard

> *(Chorus)*
> *A man has sorrows*
> *That will not disappear*
> *They get numb together*
> *To get away from here*
> *A man has sorrows*
> *That can't be repaired*
> *They get nailed together*
> *With a six pack of beer*

(Verse)
He had a woman
Didn't last for long
Fist curled in anger
Went off like a bomb

Best be alone
With tools of the trade
Two by fours & steel
To temper his rage - (repeat Chorus)

(Bridge)
End of the day
One stop to make
Headed home
But not alone - (repeat Chorus)

Laura's Refined Lyric

Laura says: I was hyper-aware that the key would be
"key" here; that I could create a lot of the tension and
highlight the irony I saw with major/minor shifts. Weird
to be singing about paradise, comics and candy in a minor
key. And each time I played it, I was able to refine lyrics
that weren't quite right or "snagged" me.

(Verse 1)
Paradise
Through a little kid's eyes
Comics, pinball, ice cream and more
In my Gramma's candy store
Newspapers came in before daylight
She closed up shop close to midnight

> *(Chorus)*
> *She smiled, and she dreamed*
> *On the tunes she hummed made her escape*

Her own hopes a tiny tied bundle inside
Of the prison of day after day after day.

(Verse 2)
Tending the line up for news and for smokes
Same faithful customers, same tired jokes
She worked hard and mostly she stayed to herself
But oh, how she longed for something else
The broken down boxes were tied up with twine
She was tied down by duty and time.

(Chorus)
And she smiled, and she dreamed
On the tunes she hummed made her escape
Her own hopes a tiny tied bundle inside
Of the prison of day after day after day

(Bridge)
Endlessly patient, good natured and kind
You'd almost believe she didn't mind

How the song evolves is a process of its own. We find it's best to not be in a big hurry to put them in fixed form. Songs are living, breathing entities and we may need to live with them for awhile to find out what they truly are. Maybe after singing the song twenty five times you'll reach a deeper connection to the song and go back and change a word or line. You might find a way to open the door a little wider for your audience. Songwriting is not a race. And songs, like people, may need time to reveal themselves. You may think that in writing the song you have reached your ultimate level of vulnerability. But in telling the story, you may discover that you have one or more layers of defense yet to get through.

Preparing for a Bigger Performance

There is a big difference between presenting a new song to a songwriting group and putting a brand new song in your set list for a professional show. Even the most seasoned performer needs to learn their song. Obviously at some point it'll be ready for inclusion, but it's a risk to bring it out too soon. DO try this at home-- many, many times-- before it goes on stage.

Practice is paramount. Work out the dynamics of the song through repetition. Vocally, are there high or low notes to prepare for or long lines that require big breaths? Vocal dynamics need to be considered as well - softer and louder parts to suit the mood or lyric, phrasing for maximum impact. The song's overall tension and release, crescendo and decrescendo and other musicalities also take time to hone. Iron out the rough spots and be intimate with the song before adding it to the whole show. Here are a few more tips to help you get ready for the big unveiling:

Practice performing the song until you're completely comfortable singing it and playing it on your instrument. It is never too late to improve a song. Use rehearsal to assess what is working and what is not quite working, and be willing to make changes to enhance message, flow, performance.

Know how to introduce the song. Never begin with, "This song is about..." A good introduction compliments the delivery of your song by putting your audience in the right frame of mind to receive it without hearing the whole story before you actually perform the piece. Introductions should set the stage and give a little background information pertinent to the story and message you want them to receive.

Relax and be yourself. If you're uncomfortable and trying too hard to put on a "persona", your audience will feel it. If you're at ease, your audience will be at ease. If you're nervous, just be honest and real with your audience. They will appreciate authenticity.

Control the environment to the extent it is possible: Nothing around the feet which could pose a trip hazard, no open window blowing in the face or blowing notes around, a glass of water, a capo, pick, anything else needed.

Allow for interaction: Take time, spread out into the space the song takes with the audience. Allow the audience the time to hear and learn and feel the things about the song. The Artists' Estate is relevant here. Do not feel apologetic for taking up the audience's time and rush through the song. The song is a story to tell; you have a right to tell it as it ought to be told, and the audience has a right to hear it as it ought to be heard.

Respond to your audience: The benefit of knowing your song inside and out will be valuable here, so that if there is some feedback from the audience, or they start clapping, or "testifying", you won't be thrown off.

We want to hear your song stories. We've created a place on our website for you to share your work with us and other readers/writers so be sure to visit ***www.mysongcraft.com.***

https://mysongcraft.com/members/

#6-Tell Your Story

"Outside is where art should live, amongst us, where it can act as a public service, promote debate, voice concerns, forge identities. Don't we want to live in a world made of art, not just decorated by it?"

Banksy
English street artist, vandal, political activist, and film director.

"Authenticity is a collection of choices that we have to make every day. It's about the choice to show up and be real. The choice to be honest. The choice to let our true selves be seen."

Brene Brown
Research professor, author

Wrap Up

We go to great lengths to shield ourselves from 'feeling' too much. This is why we've asked you to be vulnerable and authentic throughout this book. We designed the exercises in SongCRAFT to help you access the depths of memory and experience during a specific time in your life with the hope you would write a song along the way. This process, this quest of trusting instinct and emotions, is an invitation to be intimate with your most authentic self. As Oscar Wilde say, "Be yourself, everyone else is taken."

Authenticity is a journey of self discovery and acceptance. Paul Simon's statement, "I'm more interested in what I discover than what I invent" reminds us that the 'stuff' creeping out of the cracks and crevasses as we explore our lives is really where the interesting details reside. Maybe you couldn't quite get to your core; Maybe you were only able to remove the first couple of layers this time around. That's ok. SongC.R.A.F.T. isn't meant to be just one exercise. It is an odyssey, a pilgrimage to a way of being that may at times be perplexing and scary, but also offers opportunity for enormous personal release and reward. Wouldn't it be amazing if every song we write could become an exploration vehicle for our audience as well? The beautiful thing about opening ourselves up is that it gives permission for others around us to be open as well. Our purpose is to amass evidence that we were here, together, spanning the far reaches of our collective experience, offering solace, bridging divides, and creating community.

In closing we want to remind you that inspiration can be found in many places: a concert, a hummingbird in the garden, tripping on a box we have been meaning to move for two weeks, losing someone we love, finding a treasure from our childhood (the flannel shirt Dad gave you when you were twelve), and even being bored at our work cubicle. Anything we feel a connection to that can emerge from our pens with some authenticity is a valid starting point.

There are many ways to advance our craft: songwriters' workshops, retreats, online courses, and conferences that can provide a rich and deep environment within which to write and share information and knowledge with fellow writers. It is our hope that you will continue your study of songwriting and creative process, but remember that you already have everything you need to write your best songs. We need your voice and your story. The world needs us to break down barriers and trust that this work is worth doing. Follow the wisdom of Joseph Campbell when he tells us:

> *"If you do follow your bliss you put yourself on a kind of track that has been there all the while, waiting for you, and the life that you ought to be living is the one you are living. Follow your bliss and don't be afraid, and doors will open where you didn't know they were going to be."*

We sincerely hope this process has been rewarding for you and your inner writer. We can't wait to hear the work that you create using the exercises in this book.

Please be sure to share them with us at:

www.mysongcraft.com

and with the world at:

#mycreativeheart.

https://mysongcraft.com/members/

#7-Wrap Up

"The creative process is a process

of surrender, not control."

Julia Cameron
Author

"The creative process is not con-

trolled by a switch you can simply

turn on or off; it's with you all the

time."

Alvin Ailey
Choreographer

A Note About The Creative Process

In 1926, English social psychologist and London School of Economics co-founder Graham Wallas, sixty-eight at the time, penned "The Art of Thought", an insightful theory outlining the four stages of the creative process, based both on his own empirical observations and on the accounts of famous inventors and academics. In his book, Wallas outlined various stages people go through while working on solutions to problems. Now known as "Wallas' model of the Creative process", he named four stages involved in the evolution of an idea: 1) Preparation, 2) Incubation, 3) Illumination and 4) Verification. It has evolved over the years to include one additional stage called "Actualization".

Perhaps unknowingly, we have been engaged in these stages during the songwriting process. Nancy says, "I became aware of this model while working as a sign/graphic designer and songwriter simultaneously. Designing a logo for a client or writing a lyric for a love song required exactly the same creative steps - I just had different terminology for each discipline." So whether you're an engineer trying to solve a structural problem, a plumber laying pipe in a complex environment, a chef experimenting with a new combination of flavors, or a songwriter mining for the next nugget, Wallis's model is most likely working in the background.

Part of the inspiration for SongC.R.A.F.T. was founded on this model of creativity. Each chapter represents one of the stages in the process, and we hope that by expanding on them now, you will gain insight into how this marvelous system works in your songwriting life.

Preparation or Inception

This is the stage where an idea for in your head and you go about gathering information to support the concept. Here you must calm the critic and create a self-affirming narrative in place of the negative one so you can move forward. Stream-writing is a useful tool at this stage. Use it as a starting point to spill the blood and guts of your idea on the page; pinprick the callouses and let it all out. It is also the stage to do additional research on a topic. For example, writing about your grandfather who was bricklayer will require understanding what that life and trade was like in his lifetime. Or, if you want to grow the perfect tomato, you'll have to select a variety to plant, figure out the soil balance, and know how to fertilize the plant so it grows to fruition when you can finally pluck a big red juicy beefsteak off the vine and add it to your burger! We need to gather information to help us attach emotional content to the idea and make it authentic.

Incubation or Germination

At this stage, we step away from our work and go cut the grass or take a walk. It's important to let our idea settle into our subconscious by doing mundane tasks. Even the most routine assignments, like making coffee or waiting in line at the bank, gives our song idea a chance to quietly mingle with infinite amounts of information stored in the recesses of our minds. Keep a notepad on your nightstand because the answer to your most pressing problem may come to light when you're at rest. This stage can last for the length of an afternoon nap, or it may take six months to resolve, but all the while you are allowing your subconscious to dig through the fertile soil of your memory. In your daily creative practice, this is the perfect time to tenderly reach down deep a look for the emotional connection between your idea and your personal experience, like watering your subconscious. The seeds we plant need time to germinate, and it's simply part of the process to allow them to do this in their own time. So plant your idea in lush soil, put it on the window sill, add water and make sure it gets enough light.

Illumination

The "ah ha" moment! You've been nurturing physical, mental and spiritual creative space, honoring your songwriting practice and your Artist's Estate and paving the way for your inevitable epiphanies. In this stage the lightning bolt flashes and all the information you've been cultivating finally makes sense. It's the moment that the word or line you were struggling with finally presents itself and becomes the crux of the song. Or the instance you realize the anguish around the third person character in the song is really you, the tears flow and you know exactly what to do next. Wallas says illumination cannot be forced, and is in fact the product of the "germination" of the phase. Tend to the seed and soon it will surprise you with a tiny green sprout breaking free from the weight of the terra firma, to bask in the beautiful light of your brilliance.

Actualization

Here's where our work starts to take shape. This stage requires deliberate effort to test the validity of the idea and bring it into its final form. It's the point where the lyric and meter unite and details get written in a cohesive framework. You sit with an instrument and colour the chords to marry the emotional context of the song with the melody. You write, edit, rewrite and edit again. This is the 99% perspiration stage. You need to tie the tomato plant to support stakes and prune the suckers to provide better airflow around the plant. Work the soil and add fertilizer so the fruit will have lots of energy to grow and ripen. In other words, focus and organize your ideas and get that song written!

Verification

We've ironed out the wrinkles, penned our three and a half minute novel and we're ready to tell the story. But, does our song actually fulfill the criteria we set out to accomplish? Are all the dots connected or is there a hole in the second verse? Does the song make sense figuratively, literally, temporally? Testing out a new song is an exciting and vulnerable stage in the creative process. In this stage, we must be completely open to comments of our listener, whether positive or negative. We can't stress strongly enough the importance of working with a person or songwriting group who will support your efforts, offer constructive feedback and help you grow as a writer. You've done the work and now it's time to enjoy a big juicy bite of sun ripened tomato. Stand with pride and savor this delicious moment knowing you cultivated something beautiful and true.

When we are in the midst of daily work and routine, the apparent interplay and culmination of all five of these stages are working together to help you find solutions to multiple problems. Wallas says, "An economist reading a Blue Book, a physiologist watching an experiment, or a businessman going through his morning's letters, may at the same time be "incubating" on a problem which he proposed to himself a few days ago, be accumulating knowledge in "preparation" for a second problem, and be "verifying" his conclusions on a third problem." He goes on to suggest that all our activities and emotional explorations "resemble a musical composition in that the stages leading to success are not very easily fitted into a "problem and solution" scheme." It is in retrospect that we see and understand there has been a process working in the background. Our awareness of its presence, though not necessary, will prove beneficial to our understanding of setbacks and detours throughout the journey. The more we know, the better the yield.

C- Calm the inner critic - Preparation or inception

R- Reach down deep - Incubation or Germination

A- Artist's Estate - Illumination

F- Focus your ideas - Actualization

T- Tell your story - Verification

Exercise: What just happened?

Take a few minutes now, relax in a comfortable chair and reflect on how the stages of creativity were present while you did the exercises in this book. How did the main idea surface, and what did it take to make it to grow? Did you feel the critic sneak in at anytime during the process? Did you walk away from the work and to let your idea germinate? What was your 'aha' moment and when did it appear? Did you start down one road and stay on it or did you change course and head in a different direction? Did you have to let go of something you loved in order to serve the central idea? What was the biggest struggle and where were the biggest breakthroughs? What was it like to play the song for someone? Did they 'get it'? What worked or didn't work?

It has been our experience that when we can name things, like the five stages of the creative process, we immediately become aware more of their influence and activity in our day to day. We were all born with the innate gift to problem solve and create. See if you can recognize this process in all areas of your life.

Bibliography

Blume, Jason. *6 Steps to Songwriting Success: The Comprehensive Guide to Writing and Marketing Hit Songs.* N.p.: Billboard, 2009. Print.

Boyd, Jenny. "It's Not Only Rock 'n' Roll: Iconic Musicians Reveal the Source of Their Creativity." *Barnes & Noble. N.p., n.d.* Web.

Braheny, John. *The Craft and Business of Songwriting.* N.p.: Writer's Digest, 2006. Print.

Brown, Brene. *Daring Greatly: How the Courage to Be Vulnerable Transforms the Way We Live, Love, Parent, and Lead.* N.p.: Penguin, 2016. Print.

Bukowski, Charles, and Abel Debritto. *On Writing.* N.p.: Ecco, an Imprint of HarperCollinsPublishers, 2016. Print.

Cameron, Julia. *The Artist's Way: A Spiritual Path to Higher Creativity.* N.p.: Macmillan, 2016. Print.

Conner, Janet. *Writing down Your Soul: How to Activate and Listen to the Extraordinary Voice within.* N.p.: Conari, 2009. Print.

Cook, Marshall J. "Freeing Your Creativity: A Writer's Guide (PAPERBACK PRINTING) Paperback – March, 1995." *Freeing Your Creativity: A Writer's Guide (PAPERBACK PRINTING): Marshall J. Cook: 9780898796643: Amazon. com: Books.* N.p., n.d. Web.

Elliot, Carolyn. "Awaken Your Genius: A Seven-Step Path to Freeing Your Creativity and Manifesting Your Dreams - Carolyn Elliott." N.p., n.d. Web.

Frederick, Robin. *Shortcuts to Hit Songwriting: 126 Proven Techniques for Writing Songs That Sell.* N.p.: Taxi Music, 2008. Print.

Gilbert, Elizabeth. "Big Magic: Creative Living Beyond Fear" N.p. Riverhead Books, 2015, Print.

Goldberg, Natalie. *Writing down the Bones: Freeing the Writer within ; Wild Mind: Living the Writer's Life.* N.p.: Quality Paperback Book Club, 1991. Print.

Jordan, Barbara L. *Songwriters Playground.* N.p.: urge, 2008. Print.

Katie, Byron, and Stephen Mitchell. *Question Your Thinking, Change the World: Quotations from Byron Katie.* N.p.: Hay House, 2013. Print.

Kleon, Austin. *Steal like an Artist: 10 Things Nobody Told You about Being Creative.* N.p.: Workman, 2012. Print.

Lamott, Anne. *Bird by Bird: Some Instructions on Writing and Life.* N.p.: Scribe, 2009. Print.

Pattison, Pat. *Songwriting: Essential Guide to Lyric Form and Structure.* N.p.: Berklee, 1991. Print.

Pattison, Pat. *Songwriting: Essential Guide to Lyric Form and Structure: Tools and Techniques for Writing Better Lyrics.* N.p.: Music Sales, 1992. Print.

Pattison, Pat. *Songwriting without Boundaries: Lyric Writing Exercises for Finding Your Voice.* N.p.: Writer's Digest, 2012. Print.

Perricone, Jack. *Melody in Songwriting: Tools and Techniques for Writing Hit Songs.* N.p.: Berklee, 2007. Print.

Simos, Mark. "Songwriting Strategies." *Berklee Press.* N.p., 09 June 2016. Web.

Webb, Jimmy. *Tunesmith: Inside the Art of Songwriting.* N.p.: Hachette, 2014. Print.

Weiland, K. M. "Conquering Writer's Block and Summoning Inspiration: Learn to Nurture a Lifestyle of Creativity (Helping Writers Become Authors Book 5) Kindle Edition." Conquering Writer's Block and Summoning Inspiration: Learn to Nurture a Lifestyle of Creativity (Helping Writers *Become Authors Book 5) - Kindle Edition by K.M. Weiland. Reference Kindle EBooks @ Amazon.com. N.p., n.d. Web.*

Zollo, Paul. *Songwriters on Songwriting.* N.p.: Da Capo, 2003. Print.

SongC.R.A.F.T.

Made in the USA
San Bernardino, CA
30 May 2019